Emily's Secret

No One Can Find Out

written by
Linda Barr

To the many girls who are keeping Emily's secret.
I hope you will soon find the help you need—
and the good health you deserve!

Second printing by Willowisp Press 1997.

Published by PAGES Publishing Group
801 94th Avenue North, St. Petersburg, Florida 33702

Printed in the United States of America

Willowisp Press®

2 4 6 8 10 9 7 5 3

ISBN 0-87406-869-X

Chapter

One

ON Friday afternoon as the bell rang to end the school day, Emily edged into the crowded gym. She was glad no one was paying any attention to her. She knew she had no chance of being chosen as a cheerleader. Actually, she was hoping no one would even remember she had tried out. Emily was already trying to forget that herself.

You didn't keep your toes pointed when you jumped, she reminded herself. *And your arms flopped around when you tried that dumb routine you made up. Why did you think you could be a cheerleader? Why didn't you practice more?*

Actually, Emily had decided at the last minute to try out, so she didn't have much time to practice. She hadn't even told her parents she was going to try out. If she made it, it would be a big surprise for them. If she didn't, well, they would never know about it. It would be just one more thing that didn't work out the way she had hoped, like starting high school.

Emily had thought she would be starting ninth grade back in Hamilton with Kara and the other kids she had known forever. But here she was, new in town, a scared island in a sea of strangers.

They had moved so her dad could take a new job, managing a big staff and getting a much higher salary. All he had talked about before they moved were "the great opportunities" for his career.

Her mom had been excited about the move because she figured she could find a better job in a bigger city. Even before the family started packing, she had begun updating her résumé. Back in Hamilton, Emily's mom had been a bank supervisor, but now she hoped to become the manager of a whole branch bank.

Of course, Emily had gone along with the move. What else could she do? Now she was pretending to be happy at Sycamore High, but she really missed Kara back in Hamilton. *That's where I should be, too,* Emily told herself. *I belong there, not here. For sure.*

Emily's sister Stephanie was starting sixth grade this year at a new middle school, but Stephanie made new friends every time she left the house. Emily had this crazy hope that

4

if she became a cheerleader, it would be easier for her to make friends, too. And maybe her parents would come to the school games, just to watch her cheer.

As Emily daydreamed, the gym teacher announced the first cheerleader, someone named Samantha. As Samantha walked up and stood beside the teacher, her blond hair fell like silk around her shoulders. Emily knew from Samantha's smile that she had never doubted she would be a cheerleader.

The next new cheerleader, a girl named Becca, looked like Samantha's sister. She also had gorgeous blond hair and could have easily been a model. Becca glided up to the front of the gym and hugged Samantha. Then they stood with their arms around each other's waists.

Emily hoped that some day she would have a friend like that at Sycamore High. She glanced around at the small groups of girls giggling and gossiping together. Was she the only one at this school who didn't belong here?

Then the teacher called up a girl named Angela. Angela seemed like another good choice, with her big smile and sparkly eyes. She was so full of energy that she practically bounced when she walked.

The next girl, Marney, had short, shiny

black hair and another big smile. On her way to the front of the gym, she turned and held up both thumbs as a sign to her friends in the crowd. They yelled back, "Way to go, Marney!"

Next was a girl named Jodi. *I know her!* Emily realized. *She sits behind me in home-room. A day or two ago, she told me she helps out at an animal shelter. She'll sure be busy now.* So many girls were hugging Jodi that it took a while for her to get up to where the teacher was standing. It was hard for Emily to watch.

Soon there were five girls standing beside the gym teacher. Only one more new cheer-leader to be named. *You might as well get your books out of your locker and head for home,* Emily told herself. *You've got a geometry test on Monday. You're going to have to study hard if you expect to get another A. Take home your language arts folder, too, so you can work on it over the weekend . . .*

Suddenly the gym was almost quiet. Emily looked up and saw some of the girls staring at her. Had she been thinking out loud?

"Emily? Emily Davis, are you here?" the gym teacher called.

For a second, Emily's brain refused to work. Was the teacher taking attendance? No, that didn't make sense . . .

Then she realized what had happened! She had been chosen! She was the sixth cheerleader! Her hand flew to her mouth. Emily knew she should go up to the front of the gym, but she was so scared, she couldn't make her legs move. Whispers filled the gym as more and more girls pointed at her. Emily glanced at the door behind her and almost ran for it. Then the crowd started pushing her toward the other new cheerleaders. Her shock at being chosen must have shown on her face because when she reached the other girls, Jodi winked at her and took her hand.

"I mean, don't worry or anything!" Jodi whispered. "This'll be fun!"

After a short speech from the gym teacher and lots of hugging and congratulating, the other new cheerleaders left, mobbed by their friends. "Come with us, Emily!" Jodi called from the middle of a crowd of her admirers. But before Emily could answer, Jodi's friends had pulled her out the gym door.

The gym was nearly empty, so Emily headed for her locker. *I'll call Kara tonight,* she decided. *She'll be excited for me. And my parents will sure be surprised! Mom is always telling her friends about the things Stephanie does, like winning all those trophies for playing the clarinet. Now Mom will finally be able to brag about her older daughter. Finally, there'll be something special about me, too.*

When Emily got home, she was bursting to tell someone her news, but the house was empty. She knew her dad was at work. Did her mother have another job interview this afternoon? Emily couldn't remember. She was pretty sure her sister didn't have band practice on Friday afternoon, so where was she?

Stephanie probably went to a friend's house, Emily decided. *Well, soon I'll be stopping at my new friends' houses after school, too,* she thought. *I'll probably spend most of my time with the other cheerleaders, to start with.* Somehow, though, the thought seemed a little scary.

Emily sat at the kitchen table and tried to do some of her homework, but she couldn't concentrate. Finally she heard a car pull into the driveway. Through the kitchen window, she saw her dad's car, and then her mom close behind in her car.

When her parents came in from the garage, they were so busy talking that they didn't notice Emily sitting at the table with a big smile on her face. *Boy, are they going to be surprised,* she told herself.

"But if I took this job, eventually I wouldn't have to work that many long hours," Mrs. Davis was telling her husband. "Just at first."

"I have to work late sometimes, too, Annette," Emily's father pointed out. "One of us should be here in the evenings . . ."

"Uhhh . . .," Emily tried to get their attention.

Just then, Stephanie burst in the front door. "Hey, everyone! Wait till you hear what happened at school today!"

Emily wanted to wait. She wanted Stephanie to be quiet so she could tell her parents what had happened to *her* that day, but in a flash Stephanie was in the kitchen. "We had an election for Student Council," she told them excitedly, "and I won!"

"Stephanie! Student Council! That's wonderful!" her mother crowed and gave her younger daughter a big hug. "You already have enough friends at school to win an election! Isn't that wonderful, Steve?"

"It sure is!" Her father grabbed Stephanie and wrapped her in another hug.

Then Mrs. Davis noticed her other daughter. "Emily, did you hear the good news?"

"That's great," Emily said quietly. "I have some good news, too."

Her mom brushed back Stephanie's curly hair and kissed her on the forehead. "You have some news, Emmy? What is it, dear?"

Emily took a big breath. "I was chosen as a

9

cheerleader today. It's only J-V, but—"

"A cheerleader!" Stephanie squealed and threw herself on her sister. "My sister is a cheerleader! That's even more exciting than being on Student Council!" Stephanie jumped around the kitchen. "Wait till I tell everyone at school!"

Her mother's mouth had dropped open. "You're going to be a cheerleader? I mean . . . that's wonderful, Emily! I didn't even know you tried out!" She hugged Emily and put her other arm around Stephanie, but Emily could still see the surprise in her mom's eyes. "We sure have great kids, don't we, Steve?"

Mr. Davis grinned and squeezed Emily's arm. "We sure are proud of both of you."

Now Mrs. Davis held Emily at arm's length and looked her up and down. "Cheerleaders get lots of exercise," she said. "That'll be good for you, Emily."

"Annette . . .," Mr. Davis said in a warning voice.

Mrs. Davis looked at her husband. "I was just going to say that exercise will help Emily tone up her muscles and—"

"How about some dinner?" Mr. Davis asked quickly. "It's my turn to cook, and we're having my specialty—enchiladas!"

During dinner, Stephanie talked nonstop

about Student Council. When she finally paused to take a breath, Mr. Davis asked, "Emmy, how many cheerleaders are there on the J-V squad? Do you know any of the other girls yet?"

As Emily told him what she knew about the other girls, she reached for the plate of enchiladas. Her mother suddenly put her hand out and stopped Emily from picking up the plate.

"You've already had two, haven't you, dear?" her mother asked. "You're really going to have to watch what you eat, Emily, now that you're a cheerleader. You don't want people to call you the 'fat cheerleader,' right?"

Emily eyed the plump enchiladas, but then she sighed and pulled her hand back. "Right," she told her mom.

Oh, well, Emily told herself. *If I have to pass up some second helpings, it'll be worth it. This is my chance to be someone special at Sycamore High. It'll probably be my only chance, so I'm not going to blow it. I'll watch what I eat and practice a lot so I can do all the cheers perfectly. I'll be the best cheerleader this school has ever seen! And I won't be the "fat cheerleader."*

Later that night, Emily dreamed that she and the other cheerleaders were running out onto the football field to do a cheer. As they shouted the cheer, the crowd roared it with

11

them. Emily soared into the air during the jumps, trying not to outdo the other girls. When the cheer was over, Emily's friends in the stands yelled to her and waved. One of them was a good-looking guy with a special smile.

Yes, she told herself in the dream, *this is the way my life will be from now on, just as I always hoped it would be.*

Chapter

Two

THE following Tuesday, Emily rushed to the locker room after her last class. She hurried to change into shorts and a T-shirt for her first cheerleading practice. Sam's mom, Mrs. Williams, was in the locker room, waiting for Emily and the other J-V cheerleaders.

"Some of you know that I was a cheerleader in high school and college," Mrs. Williams told them with a smile. "Mrs. Adams will be busy with the varsity cheerleaders, so I'm going to be your coach. Our first job is ordering your uniforms. As soon as you tell me your sizes, we'll go out and practice on the track around the football field."

Ordering the uniforms just took a minute. Emily ordered an 8, the size she always wore. Mrs. Williams told them the uniforms would probably come in the following Monday. She asked them to meet in the gym after school on

Monday and to try on their uniforms to make sure they fit.

Then they all went outside, and Emily saw that the J-V football team was having its own practice on the field. She could hear loud thuds as the guys smacked together. The J-V cheerleaders and players practiced on Tuesdays and Thursdays, Mrs. Williams had told them. On the other days, the field and gym were reserved for the varsity teams.

"Sam and Becca were both cheerleaders in middle school," Mrs. Williams told the other four girls, "so they'll help you practice the basic moves and cheers first. Next week we'll work on some routines." Then she winked at them. "Before you know it, it'll be time to get ready for the regionals, so let's make sure everyone knows the basic stuff first."

But as the first practice began, Emily discovered she wasn't ready to learn the basic stuff, much less get ready for the regionals, whatever they were. Why had Mrs. Adams picked her to be a cheerleader? She didn't even know how to do the warm-ups!

"Emily, sit here and do what I do." Sam patted the track beside her. She had her right leg straight out in front of her and her left leg bent. "Watch me," Sam said. "Put your left foot up against your right thigh. Then lean forward

14

and reach for your right foot. And keep your stomach muscles tight. Cheerleaders can't have pot bellies, you know!" Sam and Becca looked at each other and burst into laughter.

Emily quickly sucked in her stomach, but it didn't go in as far as she had hoped. As she leaned forward, her thighs spread out on the track and jiggled in an ugly way. How did she get so fat all of a sudden?

With a sinking feeling, Emily remembered all the snacks she had eaten when she got home after the long, lonely days at her new school. Peanut butter and marshmallow fluff sandwiches. Chips by the handful. Leftovers from dinner the night before. A couple of times she had been so starved on her way home that she stopped at the corner store and bought a candy bar—or two. She had finished them off even before she got home.

Now she could see where all those snacks had gone. Why hadn't she eaten apples and celery sticks instead? How could she be a good cheerleader with all this blubber? Why did she do this to herself—now, of all times! Was she going to be the "fat cheerleader" after all?

The rest of the first practice didn't go much better. Emily wondered if she would ever be able to do the varsity jump. She was supposed to jump high in the air, with her legs as far out to the sides as possible, and touch her toes. She had expected Sam and Becca to be good at it, and they were, of course. And Jodi and Angela seemed to fly through the air. Emily had heard that they had taken several years of gymnastics together.

Marney's jumps were a little slower and lower. But by the end of practice, only Emily's fingertips were still a long way from her toes.

When practice was finally over, Emily decided not to go into the locker room and change back into her school clothes. She really didn't want to talk to the other cheerleaders right then. She grabbed her books and her gym bag from beside the track and hurried over to her bike in the bike rack.

Emily pedaled toward home as fast as her tired legs could move. But as soon as she got out of sight of the school—and the other cheerleaders—she slowed down. During practice, Sam had showed her how to do the basic jumps and moves, sometimes two or three times. Emily had tried hard, but she could see now that she wasn't going to be the best cheerleader on the squad. She might not even be a good cheerleader. How long would the other girls be patient with her? How long could she hide all this fat that had suddenly showed up?

Her mom was home for a change, talking on

the kitchen phone with her back to the door. She didn't hear Emily come in.

"Yes, my daughter's a cheerleader now. No, not Stephanie—Emily!" her mom was telling someone. "Yes, I was surprised, too . . ."

Emily didn't wait to hear more. Her mom would not be surprised when she was thrown off the team. Emily headed upstairs. Halfway up the steps, she could hear Stephanie practicing her clarinet in her bedroom. Emily bet the neighbors could hear her, too. Still, Stephanie had won all kinds of awards for playing her clarinet, so no one ever told her to stop practicing.

Emily went into her own room, shut the door, and collapsed face-down on her bed. Tears slid from her eyes and made damp circles on her comforter.

Get up, she told herself. *You don't have any time to waste feeling sorry for yourself.* Emily stood in front of the mirror on her closet door and started practicing the arm movements for the cheers. *Maybe if I practice long enough,* she thought, *I can make them sharp instead of "wishy washy," like Becca calls them.*

Emily did the movements over and over, but they still looked as weak and limp as ever. What if she just couldn't learn the moves and jumps, no matter how hard she worked? How long would Mrs. Adams and Mrs. Williams let her stay on the cheerleading squad if she embarrassed the rest of the girls at the games?

Emily felt a chill when she remembered Becca and Sam talking about the regionals. They were some kind of cheerleading competition that was coming up. Emily didn't know where or when they were, but she did understand that Sycamore High would compete against squads from other schools. And it was clear that Becca and Sam expected to win.

You'd better shape up, Emily told herself, *and fast.* The first football game was a week from Friday. The J-V team would play first, and then the varsity team. Her parents had both promised they would be there. "To see you shine," her dad had said proudly. Her mom even got misty-eyed.

Instead, her parents would see what a klutz she was—in front of the whole school. They would certainly be proud then.

Later that evening, Emily was so tired from cheerleading practice that she had trouble staying awake to do her homework. When she went to bed, though, she couldn't fall asleep.

When Emily finally drifted off, she dreamed she was trying to do a varsity jump in front of the football crowd, but she couldn't get her feet off the ground. No matter how hard she tried, her shoes stayed glued to the track. Everyone was laughing and pointing at her, except her parents. They were looking away, pretending they couldn't see her—or didn't know her.

After school on Wednesday, Emily went straight to her room and practiced the cheers and moves she had learned the day before. By dinner time, she thought maybe, just maybe, she was getting better at them. Still, she dreaded Thursday's practice.

Jodi showed up late for practice on Thursday because she had gone to check on some new puppies at an animal shelter where she volunteered. Lucky for Emily, Becca was so angry with Jodi for being late that she forgot to check to see whether Emily's arm movements were still "wishy washy."

During the practice, Emily thought she was able to keep up with Marney at least, but she knew she had a long way to go to be as athletic as Jodi and Angela or as graceful as Sam and Becca. Fortunately, her long, baggy shorts helped hide most of her fat from the other girls.

Why in the world did Mrs. Adams pick me to be a cheerleader? Emily wondered as she bicycled home. *Is she going to be sorry when she watches me at the first game?* The thought gave Emily a sick feeling in her stomach.

On Monday, the cheerleader uniforms came in, as Mrs. Williams had said they would. Emily's yellow sweater fit fine. It had a big maroon *S* for Sycamore sewn on the front.

But when she tried on the pleated yellow skirt, it was too tight. The pleats were lined inside with maroon, and a lot of them pulled open a little. *Way to go, Miss Pot Belly,* Emily told herself. The maroon streaks in the yellow skirt seemed to yell, "Look how fat Emily is!"

She hurried to get the skirt off, but it was too late. Becca had already seen what it looked like on her. "Emily," she said, "were you trying to fool us about what size you wear? Do you need a bigger size?"

"No, not really." Emily swallowed. "I think I've gained a few pounds, but I was going to go on a diet anyway."

Becca tapped her finger against her chin. "Our first game is this Friday," she said.

Less than five days. Emily tried to smile. "Oh, that's plenty of time!"

"Well, better you than me," Sam said. "I have the worst time losing any extra pounds that sneak up on me."

"That's for sure!" Becca said with a wicked smile. Sam glared at her.

Becca turned to Jodi, who was doing back handsprings in her new uniform. "Jodi? Does your uniform fit?"

"Yeah," Jodi said. "I can jump okay and everything."

"My sweater's a little big." Marney pulled it out at the sides to show them how roomy it was. "But it'll be okay."

"My skirt fits okay," Angela said as she smoothed the pleats over her hips. "But I'd better lay off the cheeseburgers."

Emily swallowed hard. *I'm the only one who can't fit into her uniform,* she realized. *I am the "fat cheerleader," just like Mom said! But I can fix that. I know I can! I'll lose those ugly pounds. Then my skirt will fit perfectly, and I'll be able to do the jumps. Even my arm movements won't be wishy-washy anymore.*

I WON'T BE FAT! I won't! And I WILL be a good cheerleader. Everyone will be so proud of me, even Sam and Becca, even Mom and Dad! Soon, very soon. As soon as I get rid of this blubber.

Chapter

Three

AS soon as she got home from trying on her uniform, Emily hurried into the bathroom and weighed herself. That was a shock! She was up to 123 1/4 pounds, more than she'd ever weighed!

If anyone finds out I'm so fat, I'll be thrown off the team, Emily thought. A prickly feeling crept up her spine. Mrs. Williams hadn't been there when they tried on their new uniforms. Would Sam tell her mother that Emily's skirt was too tight?

Please don't say anything, Sam, Emily silently begged. *This is my best chance, maybe my only chance, to be somebody at Sycamore High, to be a cheerleader. I can't blow it, no matter what. I've got to get rid of this blubber fast, before everyone notices it.*

Emily had read in a teen magazine about a diet that allowed 1200 calories a day, but she was in a hurry. She decided to eat just 600 calories a day. She thought it would be easier to keep track of the calories if she ate the same thing every day.

For breakfast Emily decided to have an orange, a slice of dry toast, and a cup of her mother's herbal tea with no sugar. She figured she'd have to be careful about the amount of liquid she drank because it would add weight, too. She guessed that breakfast would be 150 calories.

Before she left for school each morning, Emily planned, she would make a big lettuce salad without any dressing and put it in a plastic container. She'd also take along a can of diet soda. She guessed the salad would be only about 100 calories. Her diet soda didn't count for any calories, but it did add more liquid.

On Tuesdays and Thursdays, she decided, she would stick a small apple in her book bag to eat before cheerleading practice. The apple would give her energy and add only about 80 calories.

When she got home from school every day, her dad was at work. Stephanie usually had band practice or clarinet lessons. Sometimes she went to some friend's house. And most days her mom was out interviewing to be a bank manager.

Emily decided she would eat dinner right after school, before anyone else came home. That way, it would be easier to stick to her diet. Her mom was always on some kind of diet, so the kitchen was full of fat-free, low-calorie food. And Emily knew there was a big bag of skinless, boneless chicken breasts in the freezer. They were frozen individually so she could take out one at a time and cook it.

Each day she would have half a broiled chicken breast, a small baked potato with fat-free margarine, and half a cup of vegetables, like beans or peas. She would allow herself a juice glass of water. Emily figured that would finish up her 600 calories for each day. Then, when her parents got home, she would tell them she had already eaten.

She decided to keep track of how much weight she lost, if anything, by weighing herself on the bathroom scales three times a day: first thing in the morning, as soon as she got home from school, and just before she went to bed.

Emily started her diet the next morning, Tuesday. After cheerleading practice, she was already down a quarter of a pound. Her diet was working! By Wednesday morning, another half a pound had disappeared. She was so hungry Wednesday evening, though, that all she could think about was food. She finally went to bed at nine o'clock so she wouldn't eat anything else. *You had your 600 calories for the day,* she reminded herself. *Now, show some willpower!*

By Thursday's practice, Emily felt tired and a little dizzy. But as soon as she got home, she went straight to the bathroom and stepped on the scales. She had lost 2 3/4 pounds! That brought her down to 120 1/2. Maybe she wouldn't be thrown off the team after all—at least not for being fat.

Emily almost danced into her bedroom. Then she remembered that her uniform was hanging in her closet. Should she risk trying on the skirt? She hadn't had it on since Monday. Who wanted to see those maroon streaks again, shouting how fat she was? But 2 3/4 pounds had to make a difference.

Emily yanked the skirt off its hanger, stepped into it, sucked in her stomach, and zipped it up. She closed her eyes for a second, but that made her dizzy. So she took a deep breath, opened her eyes, and peaked at herself in the mirror. Only tiny slivers of maroon showed in a few of the pleats! If she could lose a little more, even those would be gone!

"Hey!" yelled a voice behind her.

Emily jumped, but it was just Stephanie

peeking in the door and still carrying her book bag and clarinet case. She was wearing an old blue sweater that used to belong to Emily and a pair of jeans that were too short for her big sister. Stephanie did have clothes of her own. Given a choice, though, she preferred Emily's cast-offs. She kept her own reddish hair in a ponytail, though. She didn't have the patience to use a curling iron on it every morning, like Emily did.

"You look great, Emmy!" Stephanie came into the room and pulled Emily's skirt out so the maroon showed between the pleats. "You look just like a real cheerleader!"

"I guess." Emily didn't feel like one. She had run out of energy long before today's practice was over. Still, looking like a cheerleader was important, too.

Just then, they heard their mom's car pull into the driveway.

Stephanie grabbed her sister's hand and pulled her out the bedroom door. "C'mon, Em. Let's show Mom how great you look!"

The girls got to the kitchen just as Mrs. Davis came in from the garage. "Sharp uniform, Emily!" her mom said as she put her briefcase on the table. Then she squinted at Emily. Her mom was supposed to wear glasses, but she thought they made her look older.

"Have you lost some weight, dear?" she asked. "I noticed you were starting to get a little chunky, but Dad made me promise not to say anything to you. All that exercise must be doing you some good! You look much better now, I'll say!"

Emily swallowed. Even her mom and dad had noticed that she had gained weight. Were other people talking about how fat she had gotten?

"I lost a few pounds," Emily managed to say.

"Good work! You know, Emmy, Dad also didn't want me to tell you what my friend Betsy said, but I think you should know."

Emily held her breath. She guessed that more bad news was coming.

"Betsy used to be a cheerleader back in high school, and she said there was a weight limit of 120 pounds for the girls. I think it must be the same now, don't you? You'll be careful not to go over 120, won't you?"

Emily quickly nodded. What if her mom made her get on the bathroom scale? She'd find out that Emily was already over 120! She had to lose that extra half-pound fast!

Her mom just smiled. "We gals have to stay trim even if it kills us, right?" Mrs. Davis put her hands on her own slim hips to remind her daughters that she hadn't lost the battle to stay trim. "You know, girls, no one would even consider hiring me as a bank manager if I were fat and sloppy. They wouldn't hire some-one to manage other people if she couldn't even control what she ate, right?"

Emily thought about all the snacks she had eaten after school and felt sick to her stomach. *But you can control what you eat,* she told her-self. *You're doing it now on your diet.*

"Speaking of managers," her mother went on, "I have exciting news! I was offered a really good job this afternoon as manager of the Longhill branch of Banner Bank. It's a new branch, so I'll have to work a lot of overtime while we get it organized, but I just couldn't pass it up!"

"That's great, Mom!" Stephanie said.

Emily forced her face to smile. *If you don't keep control of your eating,* she warned herself, *you'll never get any job at all. Everyone will turn you down because you're so fat.*

Mrs. Davis hugged her daughters. "So let's celebrate my new job! When Dad gets home, we'll go to Bruno's for some pizza!"

Emily's breath caught in her throat. Pizza? She was fiercely hungry, but there was no room in her diet for pizza. But Emily's mouth watered at the thought of circles of spicy pepperoni siz-zling on a thick, warm layer of cheese.

Time for some self-control, Emily reminded herself. "Uhh, I have lots of homework tonight, Mom, so I'd better stay here."

"Oh, we won't be out long, Emmy," her mother said. "You'll have plenty of time for homework when we get back. I know you want to keep those grades high. Hurry and change out of your uniform so we can go as soon as your father gets home."

Twenty minutes later, they were all sitting in a booth at Bruno's Pizza Place. "You must be really hungry, Emily," her dad said. "I can hear your stomach growling."

Emily tried to smile. *I'll take off the cheese and pepperoni and just eat the sauce and crust,* she decided. *Just one slice, that's all. Then maybe my cheerleading skirt will still fit.*

But her mom caught her taking the toppings off. "Emmy!" she whispered. "Don't play with your food."

Emily sighed. How did her mom expect her to "stay trim" when they had pizza for dinner? She slowly ate the whole slice, minus a few slices of pepperoni that she managed to hide in her napkin. She was still chewing her last bite when Stephanie reached for her third slice. Emily's stomach hadn't felt this full—this good—all week. She had to sit on her hands so she wouldn't reach for another slice, too.

Finally, they were back home. Emily sat in her room and stared at a page in her history book. She could still taste that spicy pepperoni and the thick, tangy tomato sauce. She thought about how the warm cheese had stretched into long strings when she lifted her slice off the pizza pan.

What she wouldn't give for another slice, even one more bite. Her stomach would soon feel empty and hollow again, like it had all week. Still, she didn't dare get on the bathroom scales. Every bite of that pizza had probably turned to fat and was on its way to her pot belly and her jiggly thighs.

Emily slammed her book shut. *I blew it,* she told herself. *I starved all week, but I'll look as fat as ever in that skirt at the game tomorrow. The one and only fat cheerleader. There's no hope for me. I have no self-control at all. There's no point in suffering. I might as well be full.*

She tiptoed downstairs into the dark kitchen. Emily could hear voices and laughter from the television in the family room. She figured that Stephanie and her parents must be watching some sitcom.

Emily quietly opened the freezer and took out a half-gallon of ice cream. Peppermint ripple. Not her favorite, but it would do. She got a big spoon from the silverware drawer. On her way out of the kitchen, Emily grabbed a bag of chips from the cupboard. *There's no point in starving if you're always going to be fat,* she told herself.

Back up in her room, Emily sat on the floor with her back against her bed. She put the ice cream container between her legs and hurried to pry off the lid. Thank goodness, the container was almost full.

Soon big, sweet spoonfuls, one after another, slid quickly down her throat. The ice cream was luscious, almost as good as the pizza. She couldn't eat it fast enough. Between bites, she popped one chip after another into her mouth. The salty crunchiness went well with the soft, smooth ice cream. This was heaven!

For a while, Emily completely forgot about the hated yellow skirt and the big game the next day. As she was scraping the last bit of ice cream out of the container, she had never felt so relaxed and content. Emily leaned her head back on the bed, closed her eyes, and fell asleep.

Then a car honked loudly in a neighbor's driveway, and Emily's eyes flew open. The first thing she saw was the yellow skirt, hanging on her closet door, ready for tomorrow. *Tomorrow.*

Chapter

Four

EMILY pulled her gaze away from the hated yellow skirt and glanced at the clock on her dresser. It was nine o'clock, almost time for Stephanie to come upstairs and go to bed.

The empty ice cream container still sat on the floor between Emily's legs. The spoon in the bottom of the container was licked clean. Nearby was the empty chip bag, and bits of chips sparkled on her shirt. *You'd better clean up this mess before anyone sees it and figures out you ate so much,* she warned herself.

First, though, Emily unfastened the top button of her jeans so she could breathe. Then she grabbed the yellow skirt and shoved it in the back of her closet so she didn't have to look at it anymore.

What was Becca going to say when Emily's skirt was even tighter than it had been on Monday? Mrs. Williams had come to both practices this week and would be at the game. When she saw how fat Emily looked in her uniform, she might send her home even before the game started, even *without* weighing her. Emily's parents would sure be proud then!

Why did she eat all that ice cream, so full of fat? And a whole bag of greasy potato chips? She had made everything worse!

Suddenly Emily felt sick to her stomach, and she almost threw up. Then she remembered something—a way out.

Back in Hamilton, Kara had a neighbor named Mandy. Mandy ate whatever she wanted and then threw up. It seemed really gross then, but now Emily understood why Mandy did it. Emily could throw up all the stuff she had just eaten and not gain any weight! Maybe it wasn't too late to get rid of the pizza, too. The way her stomach felt, throwing up wasn't going to be hard at all.

Emily opened her door and listened. All she could hear was the sitcom blaring away in the family room. Stephanie hadn't come upstairs yet. Emily tiptoed into the bathroom she shared with her sister, locked the door, and lifted the toilet seat. She leaned over the bowl, opened her mouth, and squeezed her stomach muscles, but nothing happened.

Then she remembered how Mandy said she

did it. Emily stuck her finger into her mouth and touched the back of her throat. She gagged; then her stomach muscles heaved. Out it all came, splashing into the toilet.

Emily's eyes watered, but she closed them and touched the back of her throat again. More food surged out of her mouth and into the toilet bowl. Emily looked down at the mess and heaved again.

Then she grabbed a tissue and wiped her eyes and mouth. She dropped the tissue in the toilet, closed the lid, and flushed. Her stomach and throat hurt, and she had a terrible, sour taste in her mouth. Emily poured some mouthwash into her mouth, sloshed it around, and spit it into the sink.

The room stunk, so she rinsed the sink and flushed the toilet again. Then she sprayed some air freshener she found under the sink. The room seemed to smell a little better, but Emily hoped her sister wouldn't come upstairs very soon.

Emily slipped back into her bedroom and saw the empty ice cream container, still on the floor. She took out the spoon, stuffed the chip bag in, and put the cover on. Then she tiptoed back downstairs to the kitchen, carrying the container and the spoon. Moving quietly, she set the spoon in the sink, opened the cabinet under the sink, and buried the container under some other stuff in the trash can.

"Is that you in the kitchen, Emily?" her mom called from the family room. "You're not having a snack, are you, dear? Remember that weight limit!"

It never leaves my mind! "I'll remember, Mom," she said. "I'm just throwing away some old school papers." Emily made sure the container was completely hidden under other trash. *Now no one will ever know that I finished off all that ice cream and a whole bag of chips by myself. My secret is safe.*

Emily went back up to her room, sat on her bed, and let herself fall backwards. Where were the good feelings she had while she was scarfing down that ice cream? All she felt now was sore and depressed. If only she hadn't been so hungry, so empty. That ice cream had tasted so good. Now all she had in her stomach was an ache. But at least she wasn't going to get fat.

You got rid of all that food this time, she told herself sternly, *but you will never eat like that again. You were completely out of control, like an animal in a feeding frenzy. From now on, you will stick to your diet. You will control yourself! That's a promise!*

The next morning, Emily held her breath as

she got on the scales. She was afraid to look down. How much of that pizza had stayed in her stomach? How much of the ice cream and chips? How fat was she now?

Finally, she forced herself to look at the reading on the scale. She was down to 120 1/4 pounds! Thank goodness!

Emily cheerfully stayed on her diet all day to make sure her skirt would fit for the game that night. She was awfully thirsty, but she allowed herself only a couple of sips of water. She didn't want her stomach to fill up with water and make her look as fat as ever.

Emily took a nap after school. She was tired, but she also knew a nap would help her skip dinner, one more sacrifice so she could wear that skirt. The cheerleaders were supposed to be at the school by six-thirty, so at a little after six, she took a deep breath and put on her uniform.

No maroon streaks showed in her skirt! Relief spread through her. No one would know how much she had eaten last night—or what she had done afterward.

Her mom was starting dinner for the rest of the family when Emily told them all good-bye and rode her bike to school. She practically danced into the locker room. The other girls were there in their new uniforms, stretching out and warming up.

For the first time, Emily heard respect in Sam's voice. "Wow, Emily! That skirt looks great on you now!"

Becca looked her up and down. "How did you lose that much weight so fast?" She was frowning, as if she thought Emily was trying to fool her.

"Amazing, Emily!" Marney called over. "What's your secret?"

The truth will forever stay a secret, she promised herself. "I guess I'm just good at dieting," she told them.

"I'll say!" Sam agreed.

Emily usually didn't say much around the other girls, but as she started doing warm-ups, she told them what she had eaten each day of her diet, including the pizza at Bruno's. Of course, she didn't mention the ice cream and chips—or what she had done afterward.

"You ate just one slice of pizza?" Sam asked. "I wish I could do that!"

All that talking, Emily soon found out, made her even thirstier. And warming up made her dizzy. Finally, the game started. Emily knew that Sam and Becca gave the squad class, but Jodi and Angela gave it energy. Sam and Becca had to jump higher, just to keep up with them. Marney was doing great, too. She was especially good at getting the crowd to chant with them.

Emily didn't jump real high or yell real loud, but she tried to make up for it by smiling a lot. Coach Williams was always telling them to show their "big smiles."

Emily's real problem started after the team made its second touchdown. The cheerleaders were all supposed to do handsprings after each touchdown. Emily did one after the first touchdown, but when she tried one after the second score, her arms gave out. They buckled under her, and she fell head-first onto the ground. She scrambled to her feet and hoped, hoped, hoped that her parents hadn't been watching. She couldn't bring herself to look where they were sitting in the stands.

The third time the team made a touchdown, Emily just shook her pompoms while the rest of squad did handsprings. She hoped no one would notice, but as soon as Sam finished her own handspring, she hurried over to Emily. "Emily!" she whispered. "You're supposed to do a handspring! The guys are counting on us!"

Emily smiled nervously and nodded. *Maybe Sam will think I forgot what to do,* she hoped. Fortunately, the team didn't score again, so she didn't have to risk another handspring. Anyway, three touchdowns were enough. Sycamore won the game.

In the locker room after the game, Sam's face was pink from shouting chants and cheers. "This was so cool tonight! I hate to go home." Then she smiled. "I know! Next week after the game, you're all invited to my house! We'll have a slumber party and celebrate our second win!"

Emily's breath caught in her throat. She knew a slumber party meant lots of food. What if she lost control again, like she did last night, and couldn't stop eating? What if she ate every single bite of food at the party, like some kind of human vacuum cleaner? Then everyone would know what she was really like! She started to tremble and hugged herself so no one would notice.

"Can you come?" Sam was asking everyone. "What about you, Emily? Maybe you could give us some tips on dieting!"

Emily took a deep breath and tried to keep her voice steady. "Sure," she said. "I'll be there."

Chapter

Five

ON Monday morning, Emily hurried into homeroom just before announcements started and slipped into her seat in front of Jodi. Jodi leaned toward her. "Emily! I really need to talk to you!"

Emily stiffly turned halfway around in her seat but kept her eyes on the books in her lap. "Look, I'm really sorry about that handspring. I don't know what happened . . . If you want to get someone else . . ."

"Someone else to help at the animal shelter? Hey, we need as many people as we can get, you know. What I was really hoping was that *you* could help out and everything. How about it?"

"Help at the animal shelter?" Some of the stiffness melted out of Emily's shoulders. "I . . . I really want to, but I don't know . . ."

The morning announcements were starting,

so Jodi leaned closer to Emily and whispered, "Well, I've got to tell you, it isn't just the dogs and cats at the shelter that want to see you, you know."

Emily blinked her clear, green eyes. "Huh?"

"There's this guy, you know, Evan. He's a sophomore here at Sycamore and he volunteers at the shelter, too, like me. He's really a good guy! Well, he saw you at the game and really, really wants to meet you and everything."

"He saw me at the game?" Emily's gaze dropped back to her lap, and a deep pink color began to spread up her neck above her turtleneck sweater.

The announcements were over, and the bell was about to ring. Jodi talked faster. "I have an idea! We don't have cheerleading practice or anything today, so I'll tell Evan to meet us at Bruno's after school. You can see if you like him, you know. But I hope you'll help out at the shelter even if you feel like throwing up at the sight of him, okay?"

Emily gasped and turned pale. Then she shook her head. "Bruno's? No, I want to, but I can't. Really. Maybe another time." The bell rang, and she bolted for the classroom door.

Emily made it through the week by strictly controlling what she ate. After missing the handspring at the first game, she decided to allow herself 200 more calories a day, for a total of 800. She hoped the extra calories would keep her arms from turning into limp noodles again—without adding too much fat to her hips. She still had to wear that skirt at the games.

In spite of the extra calories, Emily was hungry all week, tired even before the practices started. Finally, it was Friday night and time for the second game. The Sycamore J-V team made only one touchdown and lost, but Emily didn't care. The fewer touchdowns, the fewer handsprings she had to risk. And she had to risk doing them, or Sam would be whispering in her ear again. Luckily, Emily had finished the one handspring she had to do that night. It wasn't pretty, but at least she didn't fall.

Emily figured she was probably the first cheerleader in history to hope her team didn't score at all. But that was just one more secret no one needed to know.

Even scarier than the game was Sam's slumber party afterward. Emily really was not looking forward to that. To make things worse, she was starving after hours of jumping and yelling. *You can eat a little,* she told herself, *but just enough so your stomach stops growling.*

After the game, the girls all crowded into Mrs. Williams's van for the short drive to Sam's house. While they went upstairs to get into their pjs and night shirts, Sam's mom loaded the kitchen table with food: chips, pretzels, nachos and melted cheese, brownies, a bowl of fruit, and cans of fruit juice and soda.

When the girls came downstairs, they swarmed over the snacks, telling each other how hungry they were. Emily carefully limited herself to a diet soda and a handful of pretzels. She ate the pretzels slowly, one at a time.

Stay in control, she warned herself. *Remember that fat cheerleader hiding in your body. She's just waiting for an excuse to come out and disgust everyone.*

Mrs. Williams broke off half a brownie and nibbled on it. "I'll leave the other half for someone who can stand the calories more than I can." She winked, then smiled. "I have a surprise for you, girls. I have your routine for the regionals all planned. I even picked some music for the dance section. I really hope you like it all, but we can make changes if you want to." She smiled again to show she meant it.

"The regionals are November twenty-third this year," Mrs. Williams explained, "so we have about two months to get ready. We'll be competing against six other squads from this region. Sam and Becca know what to expect, but you new girls will catch on quickly. The routine has to be two-and-a-half minutes long, so you'll need all the energy you can muster."

Worn out by trying to get the crowd excited at tonight's losing game, the girls groaned. Emily's heart had dropped into her stomach. She could barely make it through practices. How could she do her part at a competition like this?

"If you're really good," Mrs. Williams went on, "you'll be invited to the nationals at Disney World. That's even more fun, right, Sam and Becca? Remember the good time we had there last year when you were in middle school?"

Sam and Becca traded smiles. Emily could see that they expected to have more good times at Disney World again this year. *Is it too late,* Emily wondered, *to drop out and let a real cheerleader take my place?*

"We'll try out the routine first thing in the morning and see if you like it," Mrs. Williams said. "Get lots and lots of rest tonight! Good night!" She headed upstairs to her bedroom.

Sam grabbed a whole brownie and stuffed it into her mouth. "I know I shouldn't eat this," she mumbled with her mouth full, "but Mom makes me hungry." Then she swallowed and turned to Emily. "Anyway, you must have magic ways to get rid of fat, so I don't have to worry. Tell us your secret, O Emily." Sam bowed as if Emily were a queen.

Emily clasped her hands tightly behind her to keep from grabbing a brownie herself. She could smell their chocolatey goodness. She could almost taste the thick, sweet, fudge icing.

"Yeah, Emily, how *did* you lose that weight so fast?" Becca sounded a little suspicious.

Does she know? Emily felt panicky. She had to keep them from finding out the truth.

"Well, I just set a limit on the number of calories I'm going to eat," she told them. "Then I stop eating when I get to that limit. You know, three of those brownies probably have enough calories for a whole day." *My whole day, anyway.*

The girls frowned at the plate of brownies.

"Hey, I brought some tapes of *90210*," Angela said. "You want to watch them?"

"Sure!" For a change, Emily was the first to answer. Anything to keep her mind off the food.

But when they went into the family room to watch the tapes, Marney brought along the bag of nachos and the bowl of cheese dip. After setting the food on an end table, she dipped one of the crisp chips into the warm cheese. A golden coating of cheese clung to the chip. As the cheese threatened to drip, Marney quickly stuffed the chip into her mouth. Crunch, crunch. Emily's stomach had never felt so empty.

I'll just have one chip and none of that yummy cheese, Emily told herself. But as she casually reached toward the bag, Sam glanced over at her. *She's watching me!* Instead of taking a chip, Emily closed the bag. "These chips get stale quickly," she said to no one in particular.

If Sam sees you eat like a pig, Emily reminded herself, *she's going to wonder how you really lost that weight. She's going to figure it out. They all are.*

But as Emily looked around the room, the other girls were barely awake, draped over the furniture or lying on the floor, watching the tape. Cheering had taken every bit of their energy this evening. It wasn't easy to get the crowd yelling when Sycamore was losing.

At least I'm not the only one who's worn out tonight, Emily realized with a sigh.

After Angela started the second tape, Becca yawned and said, "I've seen this show three times already. I didn't like it the first time." She grabbed a blanket and pillow from the pile Sam's mom had left for them and was asleep on the floor in minutes. By the end of the second tape, Emily was the only one awake. She found the remote and clicked off the TV and the VCR. Then she turned off both lamps in the room.

In the quiet darkness, Emily's stomach growled as loud as thunder. Emily was afraid it would wake up the other girls, but all she heard was soft, even breathing. As tired as she was, she couldn't get to sleep.

Maybe if I just eat a few of those chips, she thought, *my stomach will let me sleep. The other girls are asleep now. They'll never know if I eat just a couple.*

Chapter

Six

EMILY crawled across the carpet and reached up for the chip bag on the table. As soon as she touched it, the bag crackled loudly. She jerked back her hand. Then she remembered the food in the kitchen. A few more pretzels would be okay, too.

Emily crept into the dark kitchen, quietly picked up the bag of pretzels, and took it into the living room at the other end of the house, farther from the sleeping girls. Eating the pretzels one at a time was too slow now that no one was watching. She stuffed a handful into her mouth.

These would taste even better, she thought, *dipped in that warm, gooey cheese.* Emily tiptoed back to the family room and got the bowl of cheese. It had cooled off, and she couldn't warm it up again because the microwave would make too much noise. Still, it didn't taste bad at room temperature. The cheese was so thick now that great gobs of it stuck to the pretzels. Before she knew it, the bowl was empty.

Then she remembered the other half of the brownie that Sam's mother had left. *You'll need lots of energy in the morning to get through Mrs. Williams's routine,* Emily told herself. She went back to the kitchen. She meant to pick up the half of the brownie, but she grabbed the whole plate and hurried back to the living room.

Trying to ignore the luscious smell of the brownies, Emily listened in the darkness for a second. She heard a few thumps from the refrigerator in the kitchen, but not a sound from the other girls or from Mrs. Williams upstairs. They would never know. She stuffed brownies into her mouth, one after another, barely chewing before she swallowed.

Emily felt the chocolatey goodness fill her stomach. Her whole body seemed to relax. But as she picked up her fifth brownie, her stomach began to ache. Usually so empty, it wasn't ready for so much rich food. Then she noticed that the plate was nearly empty. Emily dropped the brownie she was holding as if it were hot. Tears burned in her eyes. *You did it again,* she told herself. *Why couldn't you just eat a few pretzels and stop? You lost control again! You are truly disgusting!*

Emily stared miserably into the dark, holding her aching stomach. She knew what she had to do. *I don't want to,* she thought. *I really, really don't want to, but I have to. Cheerleaders who are bursting out of their skirts get thrown off the team. No one wants to watch a fat cheerleader.*

She couldn't do it in the downstairs bathroom, though. The girls might hear her. She slipped upstairs to the bathroom near Sam's empty bedroom, down the hall from Mrs. Williams's room. Emily gently eased the bathroom door shut and felt along the wall until she found the light switch. She flipped it on.

Squinting in the bright light, Emily lifted the lid on the toilet. Trying not to think, she touched the back of her throat with her finger. Then she tried to relax her throat muscles as the food surged out of her mouth and into the toilet bowl. Even all that chocolate couldn't hide the bitter taste and smell of stomach acid.

Emily wiped her eyes and her mouth with a tissue. Then she ran some water into one of the little paper cups she found by the sink and rinsed her mouth out.

She had to flush the toilet. She didn't have a choice. The rushing water sounded like a freight train barreling through the quiet house. It seemed to go on forever. *Please, please, no one wake up,* she prayed.

When the toilet was finally quiet, Emily listened for the sound of someone getting up. Nothing. She grabbed a bottle of cologne off a shelf over the toilet and sprayed it around the room. Then she tiptoed back downstairs to the family room. No one had moved. In the dark, she found a blanket, a pillow, and space on the floor where she could lie down.

That was the last time, she promised herself. The last time she would lose control while she was eating. The last time she would throw up. This had to be—had to be—the last time.

I have to find another way to keep from getting fat, she thought. *Maybe I could get up an hour earlier every day and run a couple of miles before school. That would use up calories and build up my strength for the regionals. That's what I'll do. And running will be good for me. I won't have to hide it from anyone.*

Emily's stomach and throat ached. She had a nasty taste in her mouth, and she was really thirsty. Still, she felt a little better because she had a plan now. Near dawn, she fell asleep.

*   *   *   *   *

"Get up, guys!" Mrs. Williams said, jolting Emily and the others awake. "It's already eight-thirty! Go get dressed while I put out some breakfast food for you."

Sam's mom opened the vertical blinds in the family room. Sunshine spread over the drowsy girls huddled under their blankets. "After you eat," Mrs. Williams told them, "we can try out that new routine!"

The girls groaned. "Mmmm," Sam mumbled as she pulled her blanket up around her neck. "Maybe we could just eat those brownies for breakfast."

"What brownies?" her mother asked. "You girls nearly finished them last night."

"Huh?" Sam said sleepily. "Not me . . ."

Emily swallowed hard and pretended to be asleep.

But Mrs. Williams shooed them upstairs to get dressed. By the time they came down, she had cleared away the snacks from the night before, except for the fruit that was left. She had also set out bagels, cream cheese, and orange juice. Emily was just thankful that no one mentioned the brownies again.

After the girls ate, Mrs. Williams had them push back some furniture in the family room so they'd have room to do the routine. She had a tape of the music for the dance section ready.

Then the coach led them through the routine a couple of times, but the girls were so tired and slow that it was hard to tell how good it was.

Mrs. Williams frowned. "Well, your cheer is pretty good," she told them. "With some practice, you'll be able to do the jumps together. The dance and tumble section after the cheer needs a lot of work, of course. Maybe we'll have just Jodi and Angela tumble while the rest of you dance."

Mrs. Williams looked pointedly at her daughter. "But you dancers certainly need lots of practice. And you all need to put more energy into the chant at the end of the routine, or you'll never impress the judges. We have only eight weeks left before the competition, so we'd better plan more practices. Let me think."

As Sam's mom thought for a minute, Emily felt her tired eyes sliding closed.

Then Mrs. Williams said, "I'll tell you what. We'll take Wednesdays off and practice every Monday, Tuesday, Thursday, and Friday. I'll meet you at the gym on those days right after school lets out. Two-thirty sharp, okay?"

Even Sam groaned. Emily tried not to think about how hard it would be to get through twice as many practices every week.

Then they all gathered their belongings and

piled into the Williams's van so Sam's mom could take them home. They had just dropped off Becca when Jodi said, "Just take Emily and me to the animal shelter, okay, Mrs. Williams?"

"But . . .," Emily started to object. She had drunk a juice glass of orange juice and eaten a quarter of a plain bagel, but she was still really thirsty, hungry—and tired. All she wanted to do was go home and get back in bed.

"Turn at this corner, okay?" Jodi directed Sam's mother. "The shelter is two blocks down."

In no time, Jodi was holding the back door of the shelter open for Emily, and Mrs. Williams was driving away. Emily sighed as she walked into the old house. It smelled like cats and dogs, but the odor wasn't sickening.

Jodi led Emily through a small kitchen stacked with opened and unopened boxes of cat and dog food. Worn linoleum covered most of the floor, but the wood underneath showed through in places. A woman sitting at the kitchen table was telling someone on the phone about the puppies that were available at the shelter that day. She waved to Jodi and kept talking.

As the girls reached the next room, Emily could see it had been the living room. Cats of all colors meowed at her from cages piled three high. Two spotted puppies wrestled each other in a caged-in area on the floor, and a beagle-type puppy watched Emily hopefully from a pen beside them.

Emily could hear bigger dogs barking in the next room. At least, she wouldn't be tempted to eat anything here—unless she couldn't resist the Puppy Chow.

Just then, a small black puppy raced into the room, its mouth open and its tiny pink tongue hanging out. Chasing close behind with hands outstretched was a tall teenage boy with straight, blond hair. "Hey, come back here!" he yelled at the dog—just before he crashed into Emily.

Emily fell against the wall behind her and barely managed to stay on her feet. The boy fell backwards and ended up sitting on the floor, staring up at her in surprise. His eyes were the warmest brown she had ever seen.

"Emily," Jodi said with a big smile, "meet Evan!"

Evan scrambled to his feet, his face red and the puppy forgotten. "Emily! It's really you! Are you okay? Look, I'm real sorry!" He started to put his hand on her shoulder and then pulled it back, as if she was too fragile to touch.

"I . . . I'm fine," Emily whispered. She

remembered seeing Evan at school but never expected to talk to him. He was always surrounded by lots of kids, telling stories and making everyone laugh. Now her face was getting warmer, too.

Jodi grinned. "I'll go catch Skipper, Evan. Why don't you show Emily how to feed the kittens?"

He smiled and reached for Emily's hand. His fingers were strong and warm. Despite her tiredness, Emily's heart beat a little faster.

"C'mon upstairs," he said. "That's where we keep the little ones."

Cages of kittens lined what used to be a bedroom. Tiny meows filled the air. Some kittens had their own cages, while others seemed to be sharing a cage with a brother or sister.

Evan showed her how much food to put in the bowls, and they gave each kitten fresh water. As they moved from cage to cage, he told Emily how each little cat had ended up at the shelter. Some of them had been dumped, just left outside the shelter door in cardboard boxes during the night. The volunteers had found them when they got there the next morning.

Emily took one of the dumped kittens out of its cage. It was a little ball of fluff striped in black and brown. The volunteers had named

57

her Snickers, according to the sign on the cage. The kitten looked up at Emily and started to purr. "Please take me home," her eyes seemed to say. "I'll be a good kitty for you."

Emily wondered what her parents would say if she brought Snickers home. "Too ordinary," maybe. "Nothing special about her."

Like me, Emily told herself. Years from now, her mom would probably still be bragging to her friends about the time—the short time—when Emily was special, when she was a cheerleader. She wouldn't mention that Emily was thrown off the team, of course. She wouldn't want her friends to know that her daughter got so fat the other girls didn't want to be seen with her.

Then Evan said softly, "I watched you at the game last night, Emily. I really liked all those new cheers."

"Jodi made up a lot of them," she mumbled. *At least he didn't see me fall this week,* she reminded herself.

"Emily, ummmm, would you like to, uh, maybe go to a movie? With me, I mean? Sometime? We could get some pizza afterward."

"Pizza?" Emily felt panicky. "No. I mean, thanks, but I don't think I can. Listen, I'm really tired. I . . . I have to go." She quickly put Snickers in her cage and hurried down the steps.

"We don't have to get pizza," Evan called after her. "How about subs? Chinese food? Anything you want! You can pick the movie, too!"

Luckily, Evan didn't follow her downstairs, and Jodi was nowhere to be seen, probably out walking a dog. The woman who had been talking on the phone was cleaning a cat's cage in the living room. She smiled as Emily hurried past, and Emily smiled back. She knew the woman must have had heard Evan yell down the steps. *Please don't ask what's going on,* Emily prayed. Fortunately, she didn't.

Grabbing the phone in the kitchen, Emily called home. "No, Mom, I'm not at Sam's anymore. At the animal shelter. No, I'm not bringing home some sick animal. Just please come and get me."

Emily hurried outside so she wouldn't have to talk to Evan, Jodi, or the woman. She found a place to sit on the front steps where she was mostly hidden by some overgrown bushes but could still see the street.

As she watched for her mother's car, Emily wondered why everything in her life seemed to involve food now. In fact, her life had turned into a war with food, her own food fight.

Evan seemed like a great guy, but she couldn't take a chance on eating pizza with him. She might lose control again and make a pig of herself. She could see herself stuffing slice after slice into her mouth. He would just sit there, staring in amazement—and disgust.

From the way the girls clustered around Evan at school, she knew he wouldn't have any trouble finding someone else to ask to the movies. Unfortunately.

If only she could trust herself around food. *I must be the only person on earth who can't eat normally,* she thought. *What's wrong with me? Even worse, what if other people find out how gross and disgusting I really am?*

Maybe it's better if I don't have any close friends at Sycamore High, she continued, *especially a boyfriend, although there's not much chance of that happening. Then I won't have to eat around other people very often. I would die, just die, if anyone ever saw me lose control like I did with those brownies last night. Normal people just don't eat that way.*

I can't let anyone know. I have to be very careful. No one can find out my secret. No one can find out.

Chapter

Seven

ON Sunday, Emily began her morning run, two miles to start with. Stephanie got up and ran with her on Sunday and Monday, but on Tuesday her sister refused to get out of bed. It was a chilly morning, and Emily was tempted to crawl back under her own warm comforter. Then she thought about the 800 calories she ate everyday. If she didn't want them all to turn to fat, she knew she'd better hit the sidewalks every morning.

Emily barely made it through the four cheerleading practices that week. She spent the evenings in her bedroom, pretending to study but sleeping most of the time. She was always tired, with her diet and running and the extra practices. But Emily didn't fight sleep. She let herself doze off. It was her only escape, the only time she stopped thinking about food and how much she wanted some.

Not just some, lots of food.

Emily had been hungry so long that she figured it would take a mountain of food to make her feel really good again. Maybe she would eat that mountain when football season was over, and she didn't have to worry about fitting into that ugly, yellow skirt.

The J-V team won its game that Friday night, but Emily pretended to have a sprained ankle so she wouldn't have to do any handsprings. It took all her energy just to "smile big." Saturday morning she told her parents she thought she had the flu. They let her sleep away the rest of the weekend.

At dinner the following Monday, Emily sat pressing strands of spaghetti into the sauce on her plate. The smell of the oregano her mom had put into the thick sauce was making her mouth water. But she knew that if she even tasted the spaghetti, she would gobble huge forkfuls of it. Emily could see her family watching in surprise and then disgust. She could hear her mom reminding her in a panicky voice about the weight limit for cheerleaders.

"May I be excused?" Emily finally asked. "I guess that salad filled me up." She nodded at her nearly empty salad bowl. Her parents hadn't noticed that she had eaten it without any dressing. "I had a big lunch at school today. Anyway, I don't see why I have to wait and eat dinner with you. I should be doing my homework now. I've got a big report due tomorrow."

"Please eat a little more spaghetti, Emily," her father said. "I want you to have dinner with the rest of the family from now on so we can make sure you're eating right. You're getting too thin."

Emily had weighed 115 1/4 when she got home this afternoon, after dragging through another practice. That meant she had lost eight pounds in a little less than three weeks, certainly no record. And she couldn't quit now because she still had a pot belly and jiggly thighs. That fat cheerleader was *still* hiding inside her.

Fortunately, Emily's mom came to her rescue. "She looks fine, Steve," she told him. "You don't want her to blimp up, do you?" She smiled at Emily and shook her head in amazement at her husband's lack of understanding.

Stephanie looked at the forkful of spaghetti she had halfway to her mouth. She put it down. "I guess I'm done eating, too. Can I be excused?"

Her father sighed. "I guess."

Emily smiled at her mom, not her father. "Me, too, okay?"

Her mother nodded. "Sure, dear."

As usual, Emily hid in her room all evening, trying to ignore her empty stomach. I can't escape them, she thought. *Jodi bugs me at school during lunch, and Dad bugs me at home. Eat more! Eat more! You're getting too thin. That's all they say now. If they knew what happens when I do eat what I want, those words would never pass their lips again! I have to use all my energy to keep control of my eating. I don't need anyone bugging me!*

Emily pulled some fashion magazines out from under her bed and leafed through them. She bet no one pestered models to eat, and they looked great. She cut out some of their pictures and taped them to her bedroom walls. She knew her dad would see them and be reminded about how thin and beautiful the models were.

She might be thin and beautiful, too, someday, if everyone would just leave her alone. Emily decided to increase her morning run to three miles to make up for having to eat with her family.

On Tuesday, Emily went to her bedroom as soon as she got home from cheerleading practice and stayed there until the nightly ordeal at the dinner table. It was her dad's turn to cook. Even in her room, she could smell the peppers and spices in her favorite kind of food—Mexican. Fortunately, no one could hear how loudly her stomach was growling.

When her father yelled that dinner was ready, Emily slowly went downstairs, determined to take just a taste. But a taste turned into two helpings.

As she ate, her father kept smiling. "Emily, I'm so glad to see you eat like that. I was getting worried about you! I thought maybe you were sick or something."

"There's no need to worry, Steve," her mother said. "Emily is just trying to keep her figure, that's all." She rolled her eyes and smiled at her daughters. "Men! They just don't get it, do they, girls?"

Emily suddenly realized how full and uncomfortable her stomach felt. How many enchiladas had she eaten? Way too many—that was clear. Her hand shook as she put her fork down. "Could someone else do the dishes tonight?" She tried to make her voice sound normal, as if nothing were wrong. "I have to study for a big math test tomorrow."

Without waiting for an answer, she rushed upstairs to the bathroom, where she threw up as quietly as she could. Afterwards, sitting on the closed toilet with the can of air freshener in her hand, Emily wondered how in the world she could keep eating dinner with her family. Even running three miles a day wouldn't make up for all this eating. She would either "blimp up" or tear out her insides by throwing up after every meal. Great choices!

But then Emily remembered a conversation she had overheard in the school restroom earlier that day. Some older girls had been talking about ways to lose weight. One said she took laxatives. She was sure the laxatives made the food move so fast through her body that it didn't get digested. That meant her body couldn't absorb the calories. Another girl said she was taking "water pills" to get rid of the extra water in her body.

Thinking about what the girls had said, Emily tiptoed out of the bathroom and into her bedroom. She could hear Stephanie and her parents down in the kitchen, so she was sure no one had heard her throw up. Sooner or later, though, they might catch her. She didn't want to keep throwing up—she hated it—but she had to do something to keep from getting fatter.

Emily thought the girls at school must know what laxatives and water pills did, since they were using them. She knew she could buy laxatives in drug stores, but she didn't know where to get water pills. Emily decided that laxatives might be worth a try.

Fortunately, the squad didn't have cheerleading practice on Wednesdays. That gave Emily plenty of time after school to ride her bike to a shopping center a few blocks from her house and buy a package of laxatives. As usual, her house was empty when she got there. No one saw her hide the package in her room.

That evening, after making her dad happy by eating a "healthy serving" of meatloaf and mashed potatoes, Emily helped Stephanie with the dishes. Then she calmly went upstairs, knowing that she didn't have to panic even though her stomach felt really full. She had the situation under control. She shut her bedroom door, found the package, unwrapped one little square, chewed it a few times, and swallowed. Painless!

The next morning, though, she was almost late for school because she kept having to go to the bathroom. She didn't even try making her three-mile run. After she got to school, she had to rush into a restroom on her way to English, and she ended up ten minutes late for class.

All day Emily was thirstier than ever, but she tried not to drink anything because her feet and ankles were already swollen. *If I don't drink anything, the swelling should go down,* she reasoned. But she had to force herself to walk past the drinking fountains in the hallways.

On her way to cheerleading practice, Emily wondered how she could get some of those water pills. At practice, though, she soon forgot about water pills. She had to stop twice because her leg muscles cramped up. And then Mrs. Williams put her in the back row between Sam and Becca during the cheer and chant.

"I know the shorter girls are usually in front, but, Emily dear, you've looked so tired lately," Sam's mother said. "The judges want to see lots of energy. Will you promise that you'll get lots more rest? Then maybe we can put you in the front again where the judges can see you better."

Emily nodded as she tried to knead another cramp out of her right calf. She wondered how in the world she could get *more* rest. She already slept half of most evenings, but it didn't help much. She was still tired.

As the practice dragged on, Emily desperately tried to look lively. During the chant at the end of the routine, Jodi kept whispering the movements to Emily.

"I know what to do," Emily finally whispered

back. The problem was finding the energy to do it.

Then things got worse.

"You've all been working really hard, so you deserve a treat," Mrs. Williams announced. "I'm buying frozen yogurt from Sweet Temptations for everyone!"

The other girls cheered, but Emily felt faint. "Ummm, I really have to go home now," she said to no one in particular.

Mrs. Williams linked her arm with Emily's and started walking toward the locker room. "This won't take long, Emmy. And you could use some extra energy anyway."

The girls all changed back into their school clothes and, with Mrs. Williams leading, started the short walk from school to Sweet Temptations. Emily soon fell behind, but Jodi dropped back and walked with her.

"Emily, are you okay and everything?" Jodi asked quietly.

Emily forced her lips to smile. "Sure!" Would Jodi ever quit bugging her?

"Maybe you're getting the flu or something . . ."

Emily shook her head. "No, I just didn't sleep very well last night. I'll go to bed early tonight." She forced another smile but couldn't look Jodi in the eye. Then she tried to change the subject. "How are things at the animal shelter? Is that little kitten named Snickers still there?"

"Yup, she's still there. She was asking about you yesterday, you know," Jodi said with a smile. "What should I tell her? When will you have time to help at the shelter?" Jodi looked serious again. "We really do need you, you know, and Evan keeps asking about you, too."

"With all his friends, he doesn't need me," Emily said.

Jodi shook her head. "I don't know about that. He talks about you all the time, you know. I think you're breaking his heart, Emily."

Emily laughed softly. "Right!" All Evan needed was a fat girlfriend who couldn't eat like a normal human being.

When they got to Sweet Temptations, Emily ordered one scoop of strawberry frozen yogurt in a cup. *I'll just eat one or two small spoonfuls,* she promised herself. The yogurt was cool and soft and full of juicy, crushed strawberries. It slid so easily down her parched throat that she finished it all in no time. Then she had to face reality, again. Emily spotted the restroom sign over in the corner of the shop.

"I'll be right back," she almost whispered, hoping that no one was paying any attention to her. When she opened the restroom door, she saw that it would hold only one person at a time. That was good. She could lock the door and no one could come in and hear her.

After spending half the day in the restroom because of that laxative, Emily knew she probably shouldn't torture her body more by throwing up, but she didn't have a choice. That yogurt was already turning into fat in her body. She locked the restroom door and got rid of it.

Just as she flushed the toilet, someone knocked on the door. Emily panicked. The room stank and her breath did, too. As she hurriedly rinsed out her mouth, she glanced in the mirror and saw how red and watery her eyes looked.

"Just a minute," she said in a strangled voice. There was no air freshener anywhere in the restroom. Emily flushed the toilet again. Then she got a handful of breath mints out of her purse and shoved them into her mouth. She chewed them quickly and tried blowing her breath around the room. Someone knocked again, louder this time.

"Emily, are you okay?" It was Jodi! Emily had to open the door, and soon, but how was she going to explain why the restroom smelled so bad? What could she say to keep Jodi from guessing her secret?

Chapter

Eight

EMILY wiped her eyes on her sleeve. *I'll just pretend nothing is wrong,* she decided. But when she opened the restroom door, Jodi immediately started fanning the air around her face.

"Whew!" Jodi held her nose. "Who barfed?"

Emily allowed herself to look as sick as she felt. "I . . . I guess there must have been something wrong with my yogurt. All of a sudden, I got sick. I . . . I couldn't help it!"

"The yogurt made you barf?" Jodi frowned and felt her own stomach. "I feel okay and everything." She glanced behind her at Mrs. Williams and the other girls, talking and laughing at one of the tables. "They seem okay, too. Which kind of yogurt did you eat? I mean, we need to tell someone who works here, you know, so no one else eats it and gets sick or anything!"

Emily held up her hand. "Ummm, no. Let's not. I'm okay now."

"But . . ."

"I'm kind of embarrassed about this, Jodi. Please don't tell anyone, all right?"

Emily didn't like the way Jodi was looking at her. Jodi was quiet so long that Emily finally said, "Do you need to use the restroom?" She stepped back to let Jodi in. "Just breathe through your mouth. Then it won't smell so bad." She tried to smile, but she was too ashamed of the disgusting smell, the smell that had come from her body and surrounded them both now.

Jodi stayed in the doorway, trapping Emily in the restroom. Emily pretended to be interested in a picture of two little girls that was hanging on the restroom door.

"How often does this happen?" Jodi asked quietly.

Emily clasped her hands behind her so Jodi wouldn't notice they were beginning to shake. "What do you mean?"

"How often do you, you know, get sick like this and everything?"

Emily tried to keep the shaking out of her voice. "Well, only when I eat bad food. Almost never, I guess."

Emily could feel Jodi watching her.

"You know, my cousin Nicole used to barf just like this, a lot. She didn't want anyone to know either," Jodi said. "She was always tired and everything, too, just like you. But she got some counseling, and she's, you know, better now."

"That's good!" Emily tried to sound as if she cared about Nicole. "But I just ate some bad yogurt, that's all. That's why I barfed. You don't need counseling for that!" Emily tried to look calm and confident, as if she weren't lying to the one person at Sycamore High who was trying to be her friend.

"Girls!" Mrs. Williams called. "Time to go!"

Jodi stood there for a few seconds. Then she sighed and stepped back to let Emily out of the restroom.

Emily noticed that Jodi was really quiet on the walk back to school. *Please,* Emily begged silently, *don't say anything. Don't even think anything. Just forget about me.*

After riding her bike home from school, Emily was glad that no one else was there. The house was empty and so was her aching stomach, now that the yogurt was gone.

She was starving and fiercely thirsty, but she knew that anything she ate or drank would turn to fat or make her feet and ankles swell more. Now her hands and wrists were beginning to look puffy, too.

But I'll probably eat six helpings at dinner anyway, she thought, *and then I'll have to throw up again. Or take another laxative. Or both. I'm hopeless. I proved it again this afternoon with that yogurt. I just can't control myself around food.*

So I might as well stop trying.

Emily got her allowance from her bedroom. It took her only a few minutes to ride her bike to the convenience store four blocks from her house.

At the store, she grabbed as much junk food as she could carry, especially the soft, smooth stuff. Emily studied the treats in the ice cream freezer longingly, but she couldn't keep them cold in her bedroom. At the check-out counter, she had to give back two packages of snack cakes. She didn't have enough money for everything she had picked up.

In no time, Emily was back home. Luckily, the house was still empty. No one would ask what was in her bag. Still, she didn't eat any of her treasures. She smiled as she hid them all in her room, way in the back of her closet. "I'll be back," she whispered.

At dinner Emily was able to make herself eat just a little. *Later,* she reminded herself. *You can finally eat as much as you really want.*

No one will know.

Emily hadn't realized how much of her energy she had used trying not to eat. Now instead of fighting herself, trying not to gobble everything on the table, she could talk to her family. Emily asked her sister about band practice.

Stephanie went on and on about the boy who sat next to her in band. As her sister talked, Emily eyed the bowl of mashed potatoes but resisted taking another helping. *Gooey chocolate and caramel,* she reminded herself. *Sponge cake and sweet cream filling, waiting for you. And a can of soda, too. You won't be hungry or thirsty tonight.*

After dinner, Emily took her turn washing dishes and finished in record time. "Well," she said to no one in particular, "time to go upstairs and study, I guess."

Emily did study, too, for about ten minutes. Then she could put it off no longer. She locked her bedroom door, and the feast began. It was all delicious, even better than she had imagined. First, a sweet, soft cake; then salty, crunchy corn chips. Then another cake. A gulp of soda to wash it down. Emily wished that she could have bought some smooth, cool ice cream. It could slip down her throat so easily—and it would come up easily, too.

77

She wasn't out of control this time. She had planned this. It was what she wanted to do. Emily took her time eating the treats. After being hungry for so long, she deserved to feel good, at least for a little while. If this was the way her life was going to be from now on, she might as well get some enjoyment out of it. No one would know.

When all the food was gone, her stomach felt a little queasy, but she knew that wouldn't last long. Emily collected the wrappers and shoved them under her mattress. Then she quietly locked herself in the bathroom and threw up.

Later that night, Emily lay awake. The good feeling from finally eating as much as she wanted had gone down the toilet, along with all those calories. Now her allowance was gone. Her stomach ached and her throat was raw. Mouthwash no longer got rid of the bitter taste in her mouth or the sour smell on her breath.

In spite of all that, Emily felt relief. She had finally faced the fact that she couldn't control her eating. But by throwing up whenever she needed to, she could still eat what she really wanted and not totally "blimp out." This was a different kind of control. This way, no one would know how much she ate—or how much she *needed* to eat.

Emily knew she would still have to weigh herself three times a day, maybe four times on weekends. She would keep careful records on her little calendar. She had to keep checking. She had to make sure she wasn't gaining weight. If the fat started piling on, everyone would know her eating was out of control. They would see the real her, the fat cheerleader she wanted to keep hidden, the "her" she was ashamed of.

The real problem now was getting through the regionals. The thought made her shiver. She pulled her covers tighter around her neck. If only she could do her part and not let the squad down. Football season would end just before the regionals. If she didn't have to struggle through the practices and the games, she was sure she'd have enough energy for an ordinary day.

Then another thought pushed its way into the darkness around Emily. *This isn't how I expected my life to be.* Tears burned in her eyes. She tried to remember a time when she simply ate a meal, without torturing herself over every bite. Emily knew she must have done that, but now it seemed that it would never happen again.

Chapter

Nine

ON the following Tuesday afternoon, Emily struggled through cheerleading practice. As soon as it was over, she collapsed on the gym floor with her back against the bleachers. Her legs sprawled lifelessly in front of her.

Emily barely had enough energy left to sit up. Her whole body felt as if it were filled with cement. She couldn't have gotten up if the gym had caught fire.

"Emily, you know, I'm real worried about you." Jodi's voice was soft. She was sitting near Emily, stretching her leg muscles to prevent cramps. "You didn't come to practice yesterday, and you barely finished the routine today," she pointed out.

Tell me something I don't know, Emily thought. She didn't have to see Jodi's face to know she was frowning. Emily had seen that frown too many times lately. Now, though, she wondered if Jodi was more worried about her or about winning the regionals.

Jodi hadn't seemed to care much about winning the regionals at first. But then Sam and Becca kept talking about how much fun they had last year at the nationals at Disney World. Sam had even met a cute gymnast from another state, and she was sure he'd be there again this year. Emily could understand why winning the regionals was important to Jodi now. Emily hoped they won, too. Mostly, though, she hoped she could get through them without embarrassing herself and the squad.

Emily watched Sam and Becca walk toward the locker room. Sam must have felt Emily staring at her because she looked over and frowned. Then she said something to Becca, who shook her head.

"I'll do better at the regionals," Emily told Jodi. "I promise."

Jodi stopped stretching and turned to face Emily. "I'm not worried about the regionals, you know."

Sure you are, Emily thought.

"Remember my cousin Nicole?" Jodi asked.

Not her again. Emily would have escaped to the locker room, if only she had enough energy to get up.

"Nicole got so sick that she ended up in the

hospital and everything. She kept telling us she was okay, too."

If Jodi was trying to scare her, it wasn't working. Emily had to do what she had to do. She had found a way to keep from getting fat and blubbery. It was worth it in the end, even if it caused a few problems. Nothing was perfect.

"Jodi, I really am all right." Emily made her mouth smile.

Jodi stared at Emily for a long moment. Then she sighed. "Well, let me know if I can help or anything, all right?" Jodi asked in an uncertain voice. "I called you the other night, you know, but your sister or somebody said you were already in bed. You have my phone number, don't you? In case you want to talk or something sometime?"

"Sure."

Jodi didn't give up easily, that was for sure. "I mean it, Emily. Call me. I want to help, you know. And I won't even bug you about volunteering at the animal shelter or anything, okay?" Jodi smiled encouragingly.

Emily nodded and gave Jodi her best smile. Jodi patted her shoulder and headed for the locker room.

Jodi's going to make someone a good mother some day, Emily thought. *But I already have a mother. One is enough for anyone. I'll be okay if everyone just leaves me alone, including Evan.* She remembered how he had stopped her in the hall at school that morning.

"Can I come and watch you at the regionals?" he had asked. "My parents already said I could drive downtown to the City Sports Center. That's where they're being held, right? How about it?" He grinned. "I'm your biggest fan, you know."

Emily shook her head. "I only have three tickets," she lied. "I had to give them to my parents and my sister. Sorry."

Evan's smile disappeared. "Good luck anyway, Emily Davis." He turned and walked stiffly down the hall. She heard some guy call his name, but Evan just waved him off and kept walking.

He has better things to do with his time than watch the regionals, Emily told herself. *Anyway, I'd be happy if no one came to watch them—no one at all. I really, really wish they were over.*

Unfortunately, Stephanie had circled the date of the regionals on the kitchen calendar and was marking off the days, one by one. It was not likely that her family would forget to come. It was, after all, her day to "shine." Fat chance of that!

To make things worse, Mrs. Adams had told the whole school about the regionals during morning announcements one day. Now kids Emily didn't even know were wishing her good luck. They hadn't noticed her weak jumps during the games, she guessed. They just knew she was one of the cheerleaders. That still made her someone special, at least for a little while longer.

"Is this seat taken?" Sam's mom eased herself down on the floor beside Emily.

Emily pushed herself up straighter and tried to look more alive. She began to wish she had gone home right after practice. Too many people wanted to talk to her. She had a feeling that this conversation wasn't going to be any more fun than the one she just had with Jodi.

"Honey, I know you're having a difficult time with the practices," Mrs. Williams said. "You weren't here at all yesterday. Today you turned the wrong way several times during the dance. And you seem so tired all the time. Is something wrong, Emily, something you'd like to talk about? Anything at all?"

Mrs. Williams put her hand on Emily's arm. It felt warm and friendly. But if Emily couldn't tell Jodi, how could she tell Mrs. Williams? With a perfect daughter like Sam,

Mrs. Williams would be disgusted if she knew what Emily was really like. For sure, she would tell Mrs. Adams to take Emily off the squad, maybe even before the regionals. Then what would Emily have left in her life? Nothing—except eating and barfing.

Mrs. Williams didn't move her hand, so Emily had to say something. "I . . . I've been kind of sick lately—especially yesterday." She kept her eyes on her lap, remembering the day before. She had barely had enough energy to ride her bike home after school. She never would have been able to finish the routine. Emily had figured it would be better not to show up at all than to come and make everyone angry.

"I think it's the flu or something." Emily tried to smile. "But I'm better today, so in a day or two I'll be able to do the routine with no problems."

Emily knew that was far from the truth. Mrs. Williams was so quiet that Emily guessed she knew it, too.

"All right, dear. But I hope you'll tell me if I can help you in some way. We really need you and your sweet smile on the squad. You're one of my favorite people." She put her arms around Emily and hugged her close.

Tears suddenly gathered in Emily's eyes.

She had to blink them away. Deep down, she wished someone could help her. Her life wasn't a lot of fun now.

Emily struggled to her feet. "Thanks." She hoped Mrs. Williams didn't hear the catch in her voice.

Emily decided to go straight home instead of changing back into her school clothes in the locker room. Sam and Becca were in there. They'd probably want to have a conversation, too, only they wouldn't even pretend to be worried about her—just the regionals.

When Emily got home, her mom called "Hi, Emmy!" from the kitchen. "I got home early and was going to start dinner," her mother said. "We were going to have leftovers, but I can't find any. I thought there was lots of barbecued chicken left from last night."

Her mom had the refrigerator open and was moving plastic containers around, looking behind them. "And what happened to the rest of the spaghetti and meatballs I made last weekend?"

"I guess we ate them, Mom," Emily answered. *One of us did, anyway.* Emily had gotten up very early that morning and finished off the chicken—all of it. Stephanie had tried to come into the bathroom while Emily was getting rid of the chicken in the toilet.

Emily's heart had almost stopped when she heard the bathroom doorknob jiggle. Thank goodness she had locked the door.

"Steph?" she whispered as she wiped her face with a tissue.

"Open up, Em! I gotta go."

Emily quickly flushed with one hand and sprayed the air freshener with the other. Then she opened the door, hoping Stephanie was half-asleep and wouldn't figure out what her sister had been doing.

Stephanie rushed in, pulling up her night-gown so she could use the toilet fast. "Whew! That was close!"

Hurrying out of the bathroom, Emily nod-ded. That was close. It was the second time her sister had almost caught her throwing up.

"Night, Steph." Emily headed back to her bedroom before Stephanie could ask her about the smell. She crossed her fingers that her sister would be too sleepy to notice.

Maybe I should just take laxatives for a while, Emily thought. *It's a lot easier to take a laxative without anyone catching you.* Yet, she knew she'd have to take at least two laxatives a night, maybe more. One didn't work any-more. It didn't have any effect at all.

I guess I'll have to keep throwing up, she de-cided. *It's the only way I can eat as much as I really want. But I'll have to be more careful about it. It has to stay a secret. It just has to.*

Chapter

Ten

EARLY the following Sunday afternoon, Emily leaned over the toilet and stuck her finger down her throat. She had to stick it farther down now. Touching the old place on the back of her throat didn't work anymore. Sometimes, though, she could throw up just by squeezing her stomach muscles. It was a new skill she was learning, but not one she could brag about to her friends, if she ever had any.

Finally, Emily touched a place on her throat that made her gag. She pulled out her finger just in time.

When Emily opened her eyes, she saw red streaks in her vomit. Maybe it was from her knuckle. It bled a lot now from hitting her teeth when she stuck her finger down her throat. But that red stuff was probably just the sauce from all that leftover lasagna she had just wolfed down while her parents and sister were eating Sunday dinner at Grandma's house.

Emily didn't know why her parents had made such a fuss about her not coming with them. She really did have a biology report due on Monday, and the way her grades were dropping, she knew she had better do a good job on it.

Anyway, staying home was a lot easier than facing Grandma's crispy fried chicken. And the thought of her warm homemade biscuits made Emily's mouth water. One meal at Grandma's would have put two or three pounds on her. Emily would blimp up right before her mother's eyes.

And she couldn't throw up in Grandma's bathroom. The doors were so thin at Grandma's house that people could hear right through them. Even Emily couldn't throw up quietly enough to get away with it there.

She flushed the toilet, rinsed her mouth, and sprayed air freshener around the bathroom before trudging back to her bedroom. Emily opened her biology textbook and tried to ignore how thirsty and sleepy she felt.

Suddenly someone was shaking her shoulder. "Emily!" It was her mother. Emily had fallen asleep with her head on her textbook.

"So where's your biology report, Emily?" her

mother asked in a tight voice. "Grandma wondered what was so important that you didn't have time to visit her. You must be almost finished with your report by now. I'd like to read it."

"I . . . I had to read some chapters in my book first. Now I'm ready to start writing."

Mrs. Davis crossed her arms in front of her. "This reminds me of last Wednesday, Emily, when you couldn't go out to eat with us because you had to study for a big math test. Did you get your test back yet? You must have done really well, with all that extra studying."

Not daring to look at her mother, Emily stared at a picture in her biology book. It showed a cell dividing.

"Mr. Matthews didn't finished grading our tests yet." Another lie, but better than admitting she barely got a *C*, her lowest math grade in years. She hadn't studied at all while her parents and sister were at the restaurant. She had spent that time in the kitchen—and the bathroom.

Emily waited for her mother to say more, but she was strangely quiet. Emily peeked up and saw her frowning. *Why does everyone frown at me?* she wondered. In spite of herself, she yawned.

"You seem so tired lately." Her mom's voice

was a little softer as she reached out to feel Emily's forehead with her hand.

Emily jerked back, afraid her mother would smell barf on her breath. *Did I remember to use the mouthwash after throwing up?* she wondered in a panic.

"I'm okay, Mom," Emily insisted. "Honest. I just have a headache from reading so much, that's all." Actually, she had lots of headaches lately, but not from studying. They seemed to start every time she barfed.

Fortunately, her mom didn't seem to notice her breath. "But maybe you're sick, honey," Mrs. Davis said, "and that's why you're so tired all the time. Should I make an appointment with Dr. Francis? Does anyone at school have mononucleosis or anything like that?"

"She just needs to eat more, Annette." Her father stood in the doorway. "She's still too thin from that diet she was on for a while."

"But she's not that thin, Steve."

"Well, she's too thin for Emily," her father insisted.

They seem to have forgotten I'm here, Emily told herself. *I don't mind. I would love to disappear and make everyone happy, if I could.*

Her mother sighed. "Maybe you're right. Maybe she's just meant to be a big girl."

Emily swallowed hard. She could hear the

disappointment in her mother's voice. Her daughter, the ox. Her daughter, the failure. Her daughter, who would never be manager of a bank or anything else because she was too fat.

"What did you eat for dinner tonight, Emily?" her dad asked.

She couldn't mention the lasagna. They'd realize she had eaten what that was gone— five or six servings, nearly all that was left in the pan. It was better to pretend she hadn't eaten anything yet.

"Well, I was just going to make myself a sandwich."

"You don't have to do that!" Stephanie came into her bedroom, too. "Grandma sent a whole dinner for you!"

Emily didn't have any choice. She went downstairs and ate the whole meal her grandmother had packed for her. Her parents watched and smiled, although her mom winced when she picked up the second chicken leg.

Emily took little bites and ate slowly to protect her throat, still sore from throwing up earlier. She tried to enjoy the spicy chicken and buttery potatoes going down. She knew they weren't going to taste nearly so good coming back up.

"Grandma sure is a good cook, isn't she?"

her dad asked. "She'd love to see how much you like her chicken."

If you knew what I'm going to do in a few minutes, Emily wanted to say, *you wouldn't look so happy. You'd be disgusted.*

Her mom managed to nod and say, "You're still growing, Emily. And with your cheerleading, you need to eat a lot right now. You run every morning, too. That takes a lot of energy."

Don't worry so much, Mom, Emily thought. *I'm not going to embarrass you by blimping up. You'll see. I've got this under control.* And minutes later, she proved it, although her mom wasn't there to watch.

At bedtime, Emily went into the bathroom to take a shower and nearly panicked! The place smelled like barf, but she was sure she had sprayed air freshener after getting rid of the chicken dinner.

You'd better be more careful, Emily warned herself as she got out the can of spray. *If Mom or Dad figures out what you're doing, there's no telling what they might do. Watch you every second? Lock the bathrooms? Something worse?*

But she knew they wouldn't tell anyone about her, not even Stephanie. They wouldn't want anyone else to know what their older daughter was really like. Then it would be their secret, too.

Chapter

Eleven

AT lunch on Wednesday in the cafeteria, Emily was slowly eating her dry lettuce and sipping her precious can of diet soda when Jodi came over and sat down. Jodi ate with her nearly every day now. And she hadn't given up trying to be her mother, for sure.

"We missed you at cheerleading practice again yesterday, Emily. And you weren't in homeroom this morning either, you know." Jodi did not sound friendly. In fact, she sounded almost angry. What happened to the Jodi who wanted to be her friend?

"I . . . I had muscle cramps in both legs yesterday, really bad. I could barely stand up." That was the truth. "And I was late for school this morning. My alarm didn't go off." Well, the alarm did go off, but she just couldn't get up. She missed her morning run, too.

"I'll bet. What are you having for lunch

today, Emily? Bunny food again? Dry bunny food, even?"

Emily shrugged. "I like salads."

Jodi reached into her book bag and pulled out a plastic bag with a sandwich in it. Emily could smell the rye bread even before Jodi opened the bag. The bread held many thin slices of turkey, topped with a thick slice of tomato and a layer of crisp lettuce. The sandwich had been cut in half, and mayonnaise squished out the sides of the bread here and there. Emily's stomach growled.

Jodi's voice still sounded tight, as if she was pretending everything was okay when it wasn't. "You can have half my sandwich, you know. You don't even have to share your sorry salad with me or anything."

"Uh, no thanks. I'm really full already."

Jodi rolled her eyes at the ceiling. "I can hear your stomach growling, you know." She put a napkin in front of Emily and placed half of the sandwich on it. The delicious smell got stronger, and some of the ripe tomato dripped onto the napkin.

"I dare you to eat that, Emily," Jodi said. "I think you're afraid to do it."

Emily's mouth fell open. "No, I'm not! How could anyone be afraid to eat?" As soon as she said the words, Emily realized she was. She was afraid to eat, especially in front of other people.

And Jodi was getting a little too close to her secret.

"So?" Jodi raised her eyebrows.

What's the big deal? Emily asked herself. There was only half a sandwich, so she couldn't lose control and eat four or five sandwiches. She just had to hurry to a restroom right afterward. No one would be in the girls' locker room now, and it was around the corner from the cafeteria. There really was nothing to be afraid of.

Emily picked up the sandwich and slowly ate it. The turkey was moist and tender, the lettuce crisp, and the tomato juicy. The thick bread gave her stomach a wonderful, full feeling.

As Emily licked some of the tangy mayonnaise off her fingers, she noticed that Jodi had eaten the other half of the sandwich. Too bad. She would have eaten it, too, if Jodi hadn't already. What difference did it make? It was all coming back up in a few minutes anyway.

Jodi had a strange look on her face. "Pretty good, huh?"

Emily wrinkled her nose. "Well, not quite as good as my salad, but edible."

"Now what?" Jodi asked.

Emily had a sinking feeling. "What do you mean?"

"Now what are you going to do?"

She knows, Emily told herself. It was getting harder to breathe. "I . . . I guess I'll head for math class, like always."

"I'll walk with you." Jodi collected the napkins and other stuff from their lunch and tossed it into a trash container.

"Uhhh, you'd better not, Jodi. I need to stop in a restroom before class, so I might make you late. I guess I drank too much soda."

"I'll bet," Jodi said. Just then the bell rang. They had only three minutes till the next class started. "Hey, you don't have time for the restroom or anything now, Emily. You'll have to wait until after your math class."

That sandwich was full of mayonnaise, Emily reminded herself. *You'd better get rid of it real soon or you'll be sorry.*

"No! I can't!" Emily tried to keep the panic out of her voice. "I mean, I really have to go to the bathroom, even if it makes me late to class. You don't have to wait for me. I'll see you later."

Emily turned toward the locker room, but Jodi grabbed her arm.

"Jodi! Let go!" Emily tried to pull away, but the effort made her dizzy.

100

"What's so important, Emily?" Jodi asked. "Why do you have to get to the restroom right away?"

"I just have to!" But as Emily struggled to break Jodi's grip, blackness came in from all sides, shutting out the light.

"What's her name?" a woman was asking in the darkness.

"Emily. Emily Davis." It was Jodi, but her voice was scared now instead of angry.

Emily opened her eyes. For some reason, she was lying on the gritty linoleum floor outside the cafeteria. Miss McCormick, the school nurse, was bending so close that Emily could smell the peppermint on her breath.

"She's just fainted, I think," Miss McCormick said. Then she turned to look behind her. Emily followed her glance, but her dizziness returned when she saw a crowd of kids standing in the hallway, watching quietly.

"Can some of you help this young lady get to my office?" Miss McCormick asked.

Please, Emily prayed, *let this be a dream. A nightmare.*

Then it got worse.

"I've got her." Strong arms slipped under her shoulders and knees and picked her up. She recognized the blond hair first. It was Evan. He, too, was frowning at her, and his face was pale.

"I'm okay, really," Emily mumbled, but Evan carried her down two hallways to the nurse's office. Miss McCormick and Jodi followed close behind. Emily closed her eyes so she wouldn't see the other kids lining the hallways and staring.

After Evan eased Emily onto a cot in a corner of the office, the nurse said to him and Jodi, "You two can go to class now. I'm sure Emily will be okay."

"But—" Evan said.

"You don't know—" Jodi interrupted.

"Go on now. I'll find out what happened and make sure Emily gets whatever help she needs." Miss McCormick pulled a folding chair over to Emily's cot and sat down.

"But she—" Jodi tried again.

Keeping her eyes on Emily, Miss McCormick firmly pointed at her office door. Reluctantly, Jodi and Evan left.

After the nurse checked Emily's blood pressure and temperature, she looked in her mouth for what seemed like a long time. Then she felt the glands in Emily's neck.

"You're very dehydrated, young lady," she told Emily. "Your throat is red and irritated, and I noticed some sores on the inside of your mouth. The glands in your neck are swollen and so are your ankles. And I see an open sore on your knuckle."

Miss McCormick gently took Emily's hand. "I'd guess that sore is from hitting your teeth when you stick your finger down your throat. Am I right, Emily?"

Suddenly Emily was too tired to say anything. She closed her eyes. She felt even worse when she remembered that she hadn't gotten rid of that sandwich. All that mayonnaise and turkey and bread were still in her stomach. Emily could feel her fat cells swelling up. Then she heard the nurse on the phone.

"No, she's okay now, Mr. Davis. Yes, do come and get her. Yes, he should see her as soon as possible."

Not long after, Emily huddled in the front seat of her dad's car. She had never been so glad to leave school. *I wish I never ever had to go back,* she thought. *Everyone must be feeling sorry for such a loser. Or maybe they've already forgotten about me.*

She had expected her dad to fuss over her or maybe to complain a little because he had to leave work. Instead, he was unusually quiet. Miss McCormick had let her doze on the cot for a while. Had she said something to Emily's dad that Emily didn't hear?

"Dr. Francis can see you at four-thirty this afternoon," he finally said. "Mom will meet us at his office."

"But I'm okay!" Emily sat up straighter. "I just got dizzy for a minute."

When her dad turned to her, he looked older somehow. "The doctor will help us deal with this, Emily."

Deal with what? she wanted to scream. Had the nurse told her dad what she thought Emily was doing? How could Emily convince him that the nurse was wrong?

How could she keep them from finding out her secret? She had to! They couldn't know the truth! She hunched down on the front seat of the car and hugged herself tight, trying to keep her life from falling to bite-sized pieces.

Chapter

Twelve

Later Wednesday afternoon, with both parents out in the waiting room, Dr. Francis examined Emily. She was so embarrassed by his poking and prodding that it was hard to concentrate on her answers to his questions. No, she wasn't especially worried about her weight, no more than the other girls at school. Yes, she threw up sometimes—when she was sick. Didn't everybody?

Finally, a nurse came in and took a blood sample. Then the doctor left, telling Emily to get dressed and to come to his office down the hall. When she got there, her parents were sitting in straight chairs across from a cluttered desk. There was an empty chair between them for her. Her dad still had that "old" look in his eyes. Her mom's eyes were red and puffy, but she smiled and said, "How're you doing, Emmy?"

Emily nodded but didn't trust herself to speak. What was going to happen here? Did the doctor know her secret now? Would her parents be so disgusted when they found out the truth about her that they wouldn't even want her to come home with them? Lucky for them, they still had one normal daughter, someone who didn't embarrass them, someone they could be proud of. Someone they could trust.

Emily sat in the empty chair. Her mom reached for her hand, but Emily pulled it back. She didn't want her mom to know she was trembling.

Dr. Francis came in, closed the door, and sat in the leather chair behind his desk. He smiled and talked directly to Emily.

"Emily, I've checked you over to see why you fainted at school today, but I think you know the reason."

Emily swallowed hard. This could be bad, very bad. Her shaking got worse. She hoped no one could see it.

"My guess is that you have an eating disorder that is threatening your health," Dr. Francis said.

Emily felt light-headed, as if she might faint again.

"But she's not really that thin," her mom pointed out.

Dr. Francis opened a folder he had brought in with him and looked at some papers in it. "That's true. Emily's only a few pounds under what she should weigh for her height and age. But according to her records from the doctor in Hamilton, she weighs about six pounds less than she did a year ago. She should be gaining weight at this age, not losing it."

He closed the folder and looked at her parents. "Emily actually looks heavier than she is because the glands under her jaw are swollen. They make her face seem a little chubby. Still, her weight doesn't matter. You don't have to be really skinny to have an eating disorder."

Her father shook his head. "She was on a diet for a while, but I know she's been eating more lately."

"But what happens after you eat, Emily?" the doctor asked softly.

Emily swallowed again and stared at the leafy pattern in his carpet. The seconds dragged by as he waited for her to answer. Finally, he said, "You purge yourself of the food, right, Emily? You throw up to get rid of whatever you ate."

Emily could feel her mother jerk in shock.

"The school nurse didn't say anything about throwing up," her dad blurted out.

Emily felt the blood drain from her face. The

darkness wasn't very far away now. She pushed on the arms of the chair to keep from falling forward. Dr. Francis quickly filled a paper cup from a container of bottled water behind his desk and handed it to her.

"Take a few deep breaths, Emily, and sip this. Dehydration is a big part of the problem here," he explained to her parents. "Throwing up gets rid of water that the body needs. When the body runs low on water, the person becomes weak and dizzy. She might have trouble concentrating and even faint, like Emily did today."

Emily took a few sips, and the darkness retreated again. "But I'm not dehydrated," she whispered. "My body has too much water! It makes my feet and ankles swell up."

"That's how your body tries to keep the water it needs," he told her. "It's called 'rebound water retention.' Unfortunately, the water accumulates where it doesn't do much good. Throwing up also robs the body of electrolytes."

Emily's head was full of fog. What were electrolytes?

"Electrolytes include potassium, sodium, and chloride," Dr. Francis said. "Your heart needs them so it can work right. I can already hear some minor problems in your heartbeat, Emily.

That blood sample will tell us more about how much your heart has been affected."

"Her heart?" her mom said. Emily could hear the panic in her voice. "Emily's having problems with her heart?"

"They are minor right now," Dr. Francis told her. "They could get worse, though, if this continues. But nearly all of the physical problems Emily is experiencing will disappear when she begins to eat a normal diet again."

But the fat will reappear, Emily told herself. *The doctor can ignore that, but I can't. Mom won't, either.*

"Dehydration, weakness, fainting, swollen glands, the sore on her hand—they're all signs of bulimia. That's what your disorder is called, Emily," Dr. Francis explained. "Bulimia is characterized by bingeing and purging—by eating too much and then vomiting up the food to avoid gaining weight."

Emily hated to hear him say it out loud. She slid lower in her chair.

"Eating too much?" said her dad. "I think you're mistaken there, Doctor. Emily almost never eats more than she should. In fact, she usually eats a lot less."

Emily knew her father still hoped that the doctor was wrong, that his daughter was normal.

Dr. Francis nodded. "You may never see her binge, but that doesn't mean it doesn't happen, right, Emily? Maybe even in the middle of the night?" He turned to her parents. "Has any food mysteriously disappeared at your house?"

Her mom shook her head in disbelief. "All those missing leftovers?" she asked. "Emily ate them at night?"

Emily kept her eyes down. Her face was on fire with shame, but there was nothing she could say. Now her parents knew she sneaked around while they were asleep, stealing food from her own family, gobbling everything she could find, and then throwing it all up. She was a pitiful excuse for a daughter.

"I'll bet your stomach aches a lot, Emily," Dr. Francis said, "and your throat hurts all the time. It might even bleed from throwing up so often."

Emily remembered the red streaks she had seen in her vomit a few times lately. Was that blood from her throat?

"And stomach acid has already caused sores in your mouth. If you keep throwing up, the acid will start eroding the enamel off your teeth, and you'll end up with lots of cavities," Dr. Francistold her.

"Cavities?" her dad asked. "Because of throwing up?"

Dr. Francis nodded. "Stomach acid is a powerful substance. So are laxatives."

Tears stung Emily's eyes as she sank still lower in her chair. Was there anything he didn't know?

"Some dieters think laxatives will move food through their bodies quickly, so it won't be digested," he said. "But laxatives work in the large intestine, after digestion takes place, after the body has absorbed most of the calories and nutrients in the food. Laxatives help get rid of waste material in the intestines, but they also make the body lose even more water and become more dehydrated.

"And after a while," he continued, "the intestines get kind of addicted to laxatives. They get lazy. The person has to take a laxative to make them work at all, to have a bowel movement. After a while, just one laxative won't work. You have to take two or more—sometimes many more, right, Emily? When I pressed on your lower abdomen, I could tell that you're constipated, probably from over-using laxatives."

Emily's cheeks were wet now. She felt naked and limp. She had no secrets left. Still, her mom had her arm around her, and her dad held her hand tightly. Why? Couldn't they see she wasn't worth it? She wouldn't blame them if they got up and went home without her.

"What about diuretics—water pills?" Dr. Francis asked. "They're particularly dangerous because they're designed to strip the body of water. Have you tried those, Emily?"

"No, never!" she blurted out.

No one else spoke. Her words seemed to hang in the air. She wasn't sure anyone believed her. Why should they?

More moments passed, and still no one spoke. Emily guessed they were waiting for her to say something.

Finally, she took a deep breath. "But . . . well, maybe I do throw up sometimes," she admitted in a tiny voice, "but I didn't know it was causing so many problems. I'll stop. I don't want to be sick. I just won't do it anymore."

She knew that was what they wanted to hear, but she wasn't sure she meant it. If she stopped throwing up, how would she keep the fat off? The doctor knew about the laxatives, too. How was she going to keep from blimping up?

Her mom kept her arm around Emily but covered her face with her other hand. Emily could see her shoulders shake. Her dad pushed his lips together tightly.

"I'm sorry. Really sorry," Emily whispered. "But you don't have to worry about me anymore.

I'll stop. I'll be okay now."

Dr. Francis wrote something on a slip of paper and handed it to Emily's mother. "Here's the name of a center that I've worked with before. The counselors there understand eating disorders, and I'm sure they can help Emily."

Then he took Emily's hands in his. "My dear, you are dealing with a serious problem. I'm going to ask your counselor to send me a report every week or so. I want to know how you're getting along because I care what happens to you, young lady."

Her father sighed. "So do we. So do we. We'll make sure she gets the help she needs."

"Should . . . should we tell the school about this?" Mrs. Davis asked. "They're going to wonder why she fainted." Emily knew what her mom hoped the doctor would say.

Dr. Francis thought for a minute. Finally he said to Emily, "I'm pretty sure you would rather not tell anyone else about this problem, right?" He waited for her to nod. "Then let's see if we can handle it without getting the school involved. I'll give you a note for the nurse, since she already figured out what was wrong. I'll tell her you're going for counseling and ask her not to mention your problem to anyone at this point.

"School nurses are usually good at keeping secrets," he said, "although the school may require her to put a note in your confidential record, just in case you have problems at school again and she's not available. Then whoever takes care of you will have a better idea of what is wrong.

"But, Emily, if things do not go well, we will have to contact the school and especially your cheerleading coach. Understood?"

She nodded again. She knew what would happen if Mrs. Williams and Mrs. Adams found out. She'd be thrown off the squad, even after all she had done to keep her weight down. She couldn't let that happen!

I have to stop throwing up, Emily decided. *But how can I? I'll turn into a blubbery pig! I can't just starve all the time. I need to eat. I have to eat! Plates of food, mountains of food. Even when my stomach is so full it feels like bursting, I still want more.*

What am I going to do? she asked herself on the way home from the doctor's office. Her parents sat in the front seat of the car, staring straight ahead. Neither one said anything, but she guessed they were both wondering what they had done to deserve a daughter like her.

I'm trying, she wanted to tell them. *I'm trying to be a daughter you can be proud of.*

I'm trying to be someone special, someone thin, someone you can brag about to your friends, someone perfect. Just give me another chance! Maybe I can stop throwing up. Maybe I can find a way to control myself around food.

I'll try. I really will.

Chapter

Thirteen

At dinner that evening, Emily did her best to eat a normal amount. She had to prove she didn't need the counselor Dr. Francis had suggested. She could handle this on her own.

During the meal, Stephanie talked on and on about being chosen that day for the marching band. When she stopped to take a drink of milk, she finally realized that no one else was talking—or listening.

"What's wrong?" Stephanie asked. "Everyone's so quiet tonight. Aren't you glad I was picked for the marching band?"

"Sure we are," her dad said. "We're really proud of you, as always. We've just had a hard day. Everyone's tired."

"Everyone?" Stephanie looked at her mom and sister in confusion. Just then, the phone rang in the kitchen.

"You can answer it, Steph," her mother said.

Usually phone calls were not allowed during dinnertime, but tonight was different, for sure. Soon they heard Stephanie chattering away on the kitchen phone about marching band.

"Emily," her dad said quietly, "we've scheduled an appointment for you at the center Dr. Francis told us about. It's next Wednesday at three-thirty. We were lucky to get it on the afternoon when you don't have cheerleading practice. Mom and I will be talking with your counselor, too."

Emily almost choked on the bread she was chewing. "But I'm eating!"

"Just go one time, honey," her mother said softly. "It's only for an hour. If you really hate it, you don't have to go back."

"Annette," her dad said in a warning voice, but Mrs. Davis wouldn't look at him.

Emily swallowed the gob of bread. "All right. One time. I'll go once." *If that's what it takes to make you happy,* she told herself. *If that's what it takes to convince you I'm okay.* She was pretty sure she could talk to a counselor for an hour and seem like a normal person. She didn't think the counselor would give her anything to eat. Without any food around, she could do okay. She could pretend to be normal.

"We just don't want you to make yourself sick, honey," her dad said softly.

Emily nodded and, without thinking, took another helping of scalloped potatoes and ate them in big bites, barely chewing.

"You're certainly eating well tonight, Emmy," her mom said.

Emily smiled a little, as if she thought she was eating well, too. But a chill went up her back. *You're eating like a pig,* she told herself. *And right in front of Mom and Dad! Any second now, Mom is going to bring up that weight limit again.*

Suddenly Emily wanted to stuff another slice of bread in her mouth, maybe two or three or four slices, but she knew her parents were watching. Instead, she forced herself to eat one slice as slowly as she could manage. She finished it in three bites.

"Just because of what happened today, you won't forget that weight limit for cheerleaders, will you, dear?" Mrs. Davis asked. She reached over and patted Emily's hand.

Emily pulled her hand out of her mother's reach. "I won't forget, Mom," she managed to say. "Ummmm, I think it's Steph's turn to do the dishes tonight. I'm going upstairs to finish my book report for tomorrow, okay?" Without waiting for an answer, she got up and headed for the stairs.

"Emily, you won't . . . you won't . . .?" her

dad called to her.

You won't throw up, Emily silently finished his sentence for him. She knew he just couldn't bring himself to say it out loud.

"No, Dad! I told you I wouldn't, didn't I?" Emily yelled crossly over her shoulder as she hurried up the steps.

A few minutes later, Emily quietly let herself out of the upstairs bathroom. She could hear Stephanie still yakking on the phone in the kitchen and her parents talking in low voices in the dining room. Thank goodness no one had followed her upstairs.

She went into her bedroom, shut the door, and threw herself face-down on her bed. Her stomach hurt, her throat was raw, her breath stunk, and she felt a headache coming on. Tears ran down her cheeks and made damp spots on her comforter.

I did try, Mom and Dad, but it's impossible. I do want you to be proud of me, but I can't stop eating. Don't think of throwing up as making myself sick. Think of it as making myself thin—the thin, perfect daughter you always wanted.

It took a lot of begging, but Emily finally convinced her parents to let her stay home from school the next day, Thursday. She would eat, she promised, and she would not throw up, ever again. And she would talk to the counselor the following Wednesday. But she just couldn't go back to school and face everyone so soon. Yes, she would go to school on Friday. Just not today, please.

As soon as her parents and sister left, Emily took her morning run, which turned out more like a walk. Then she spent most of the morning sleeping. For lunch, she ate her usual dry salad. When it was gone, she was still starving, as usual.

Both of her parents had already called to check on her. She kept thinking about how they had hugged her yesterday in the doctor's office, even after they found out her awful secret. How could they still love her?

Emily opened the refrigerator and saw a plate of leftover baked chicken, but she knew her parents would miss that. In the freezer, though, she found half a loaf of pumpkin bread and a box of ice cream bars. She put the bread in the microwave to defrost while she ate the ice cream bars, but there were only three bars left in the box, so the bread was still half-frozen when she ate it. Then she spotted a box of wheat crackers in the back of the pantry. No one would miss those—or the peanut butter she generously spread on each of them.

Afterwards, she buried the empty ice cream

and cracker boxes in the kitchen trash can. Then, full of food, Emily couldn't resist the temptation to lie down on the couch for a blissful nap. When the phone rang and woke her up, though, she checked her watch and panicked. She had been asleep for nearly half an hour. All that food was digesting in her stomach! Letting the answering machine get the phone, she hurried upstairs to the bathroom.

What her parents didn't know wouldn't hurt them—or her either, despite what they thought. After all, she wasn't going to throw up her whole life. Just until she got her weight under control. Maybe just while she was a cheerleader, so she wouldn't go over the weight limit and be thrown off the team. Mrs. Williams still hadn't weighed them, but that didn't mean she wouldn't do it, maybe even at the next practice.

Emily was rinsing out her mouth when the phone rang again. She heard the answering machine come on again. The first time the caller had hung up, but this time, someone was leaving a message. It was Evan, and she could tell by the noise in the background that he was calling from the pay phone near the school cafeteria.

"I guess you must be sleeping," he said. "Well, I don't want to bother you. I just hope you're okay. I've been thinking about you, hoping you aren't too sick." He was quiet for a second, and Emily thought he had hung up. Then he said, "Maybe . . . maybe I'll see you at school tomorrow. Bye, Emily."

Evan sure was a nice guy, Emily had to admit. He took care of homeless animals and checked on weird girls. *I'm sure he feels sorry for all of us,* she thought.

Just after three o'clock, Stephanie burst in the front door. "Boy, are you lucky you got to stay home today, Emmy! What a boring day I had! And we don't even have band practice on Thursday." Stephanie opened the refrigerator door. "Why did Mom and Dad let you stay home, anyway?"

"I . . . I had some bad cramps this morning," Emily lied. "I feel better now."

Stephanie pulled the plate of leftover chicken out of the refrigerator and smiled at her sister. "I'm going to start my period pretty soon, too! I just know it. You'll be the first one I tell, Emmy!"

Emily smiled and left Stephanie gnawing on a chicken leg in the kitchen. Even cold, the chicken smelled really good. Emily's stomach, empty again, growled, but she knew she would wolf down the whole plate if she even took one bite.

About half an hour later, the doorbell rang. Emily opened the door, but she wasn't especially happy to see Jodi standing there. She hadn't forgotten that Jodi had tried to keep her from getting to the restroom the day before.

"Hi," Jodi said uncertainly. "I thought I'd stop after practice and, you know, see how you're feeling and everything."

"I'm lots better," Emily said coolly. She knew she should invite Jodi in, but Jodi would probably just start talking about her cousin Nicole again. Or the regionals. They were only four weeks from Saturday now, looming like a fat, black cloud.

Emily didn't know how she would get through the regionals, especially since she had missed practice again today. But she had to get through them somehow. She had already let her parents down. She couldn't do it again. And Sam and the other girls were determined to win. They would hate her if she blew it for them.

"Did you go to the doctor or anything to see, you know, why you passed out?" Jodi asked.

Jodi sure is nosy, Emily told herself.

"I went to the doctor, but I'm okay now." Lying was getting easier and easier.

"So everything's okay?" Jodi was staring at

Emily now. Some of the anger from the day before was back in her voice.

"Yup." Emily waited for Jodi to say more. When she just kept staring, Emily started to close the door. "I guess I'll see you at school tomorrow," she told Jodi.

Jodi put out her hand so Emily couldn't shut the door. "Ummmm, Emily, is either one of your parents home?"

"No, they trust me to stay home by myself sometimes." Emily blurted out. She couldn't help feeling a little angry herself. Who did Jodi think she was, anyway?

"I just want to help, you know," Jodi whispered. "I'm scared for you."

Emily suddenly noticed that Jodi's eyes were shiny with tears. Maybe Jodi did care about her after all, and not just about the regionals.

"I'm fine, Jodi. Really." Emily opened the door all the way. "C'mon in. You can meet my sister. She's here."

But Stephanie wasn't in the kitchen anymore.

"Maybe she's upstairs," Emily said. As they passed the upstairs bathroom, the door was closed, but they heard an unmistakable sound. Stephanie was in there, throwing up.

Emily yanked open the door. Stephanie was

leaning over the toilet, gagging.

Emily hurried to her and brushed wisps of her hair back from her damp face. "Are you sick, Steph? What's the matter?"

Stephanie wiped her mouth with toilet paper. The room was filled with the sour smell of vomit that had started out as spicy chicken.

Stephanie looked confused. "I'm not sick, Emily. But you . . . and I thought . . ."

"I . . .?" Then Emily realized what Stephanie meant, what Stephanie was doing. She sagged against the bathroom wall, slipping down until she was sitting on the floor.

"Emmy, don't be mad at me," Stephanie begged. "Please. I just want to be like you."

"Don't, Steph. Don't be like me," Emily whispered. She reached up for Stephanie's hand and pulled her down beside her.

Jodi flushed the toilet. Stephanie looked up in surprise, as if she had just realized that Jodi was there.

"I'm Jodi," Jodi said quietly. "One of Emily's friends and everything."

"How long . . .," Emily started to ask her sister, but she didn't want to know. She remembered thinking a couple of times that the smell in the bathroom was from her. It must have been Stephanie, imitating her big sister.

"I should have been paying more attention,

Steph." Emily hugged her sister close. "Then I would have known. Then I would have told you not to."

"You both can stop doing this, you know," Jodi said softly.

Stephanie nodded, but Emily's eyes went wide. "I can't! I'll get fat, so fat and blubbery you won't even recognize me. You won't like me, for sure. No one will. I won't be a cheerleader anymore! I won't be anything." Emily started to cry. "I can't stop!"

Stephanie stared at her sister, and tears filled her eyes. "Then I can't either." She turned to Jodi. "We have to throw up or we'll get fat."

Now Emily grabbed Stephanie by her shoulders. "No! You have to stop, Steph! Everybody likes you just the way you are. You aren't fat. You're perfect. You don't have to change. Just me! I have to be better than I am."

"Not for me, Emmy."

Stephanie hugged her sister tight. Jodi sat down on floor beside Emily. "Emily, the only thing you have to change is the way you eat. It's killing you."

Emily wiped her wet face with her sleeve and sighed. "All I think about is eating," she admitted. "Sometimes I get so hungry that I kind of . . . kind of . . . lose control."

"You mean you eat a lot, right?" Jodi asked. "Way more than you should?"

Emily nodded miserably.

"Nicole did, too, you know, but no one realized it for a long time. Once she ate a whole cake my aunt had baked for her card club. When food kept disappearing, my aunt thought Nicole's brother was feeding all his friends after school or something. He kept saying he wasn't, you know, but my aunt didn't believe him. She never guessed it was Nicole."

Emily sighed again and turned to Stephanie. "It's a good thing you never make a pig of yourself like that." Then she looked at her sister sharply. "You don't, do you?"

Her sister, wide-eyed, shook her head. "I didn't know you did that, Emily. I never saw you. Why do you do that?"

"I . . . I get really hungry, but I . . . I'm not sure . . ." Emily stared at the floor. "I'm going to a counselor next Wednesday. Maybe I'll find out then."

"Thank goodness!" Jodi said. "Then your parents do know."

Emily nodded tiredly. "The doctor told them yesterday." She turned to Stephanie. "If I stop throwing up, will you?"

Stephanie's face brightened. "Sure! It hurts and it smells awful!" She rubbed her stomach.

"I only did it 'cause you did, Emmy."

"Then I'll stop. I promise. So you can stop, too, okay?" Emily would say anything to keep her sister from getting caught in the same mess she was in.

"Yes!" Stephanie squeaked as she hugged her sister again.

Emily glanced over at Jodi. The look in Jodi's eyes said, "I'll bet."

Chapter

Fourteen

ON Friday morning Emily weighed 115 3/4. She couldn't understand why she still weighed so much despite throwing up nearly every other day—or every other night—whenever she gave in and ate as much as she wanted. *What do I have to do to lose more of this fat?* she wondered.

Emily had considered drinking some extra water before the game Friday night, just in case Dr. Francis had been right about dehydration causing weakness. But she weighed too much to drink anything at all. She still had to wear that skirt, so she would just have to risk dehydration.

The other cheerleaders had all heard about her fainting, of course, but they didn't know why, except for Jodi. As far as Emily could tell, Jodi hadn't told anyone, and her parents hadn't either. Mrs. Williams and the other cheerleaders seemed to believe her story about having the flu. They all kept telling her to take it easy. All except Becca, who wouldn't even look at her.

The J-V football team lost the game that night. Whenever Sycamore came close to scoring, Emily pretended she had to use the restroom or made some other excuse to leave the field so she wouldn't be forced to try a handspring. Sycamore scored twice, but she managed to be in the locker room both times. Distracted by the exciting game, the other girls, even Jodi, didn't seem to notice what she was doing.

On Saturday morning, a neighbor called and asked Emily to baby-sit that evening. After Emily put their little boy to bed, she found all kinds of food she didn't think the family would miss, including two dozen brownies tucked way in back of their freezer and a bag of candy bars they had bought for Halloween.

I need to baby-sit here more often, she told herself. She made sure to spray lots of air freshener in their bathroom when she was done getting rid of her feast.

It was getting harder to find food at home that she could eat without making her parents suspicious. Only Stephanie seemed to believe Emily's promise not to throw up again. Sunday morning, Emily caught her mom doing a sniff test in the upstairs bathroom, but she pretended not to notice. *It's a good thing Mom's not checking the neighbor's bathroom,* she thought.

On Monday, though, no one paid any attention when Emily went straight upstairs after dinner. She guessed that her dad had convinced her mom to trust her not to throw up anymore. But the more Emily thought about the way she was sneaking around and lying to them, the more she wanted something to eat. Lots to eat. Sitting in her room, all she could think about was food.

By eight o'clock, Emily couldn't stand it any more. She told her parents she was going to walk to Jodi's house to get some notes for English. Instead, she spent that week's allowance on junk food at the convenience store. She ate it on the way home and threw up as soon as she got back upstairs. Luckily, Jodi hadn't called while she was gone.

At dinner on Tuesday night, the double fudge ice cream her dad was scooping out for dessert looked luscious, but Emily told him she didn't want any. She knew she wouldn't be able to stop with just one dish. *Later,* she promised herself, *when no one is watching to see if you go into the bathroom afterward. Then you can really enjoy that ice cream—all that's left—*

and not get fat.

So she waited. After everyone was asleep, Emily tiptoed downstairs to the kitchen and finished it off.

Finally, Wednesday and her counseling appointment arrived. The counselor turned out to be a young woman named Cassie. Her office was in a mental health center, actually a big old house not far from the school. Soon after the Davises filled out some forms in the waiting/living room, Cassie led Emily upstairs.

Cassie's kind, brown eyes reminded Emily of Evan's. She was about as tall as Emily and had short, curly, blondish-brown hair. Cassie was wearing jeans, a turtleneck sweater, and a plaid vest. Emily could see that she wasn't at all overweight. *Another perfect person,* Emily told herself nervously. *How could she ever understand me?*

Cassie's office had a desk with a computer on it and a wooden chair behind it. A file cabinet sat in one corner, and two comfortable chairs faced each other around a little table. Emily could tell it used to be a child's bedroom. The fading wallpaper was full of clowns and circus animals.

Cassie invited Emily to sit in one of the chairs, and she sat in the other one. After going over a form Emily's parents had filled out, Cassie got to the point.

"People with bulimia go in circles," she explained. "First, they starve themselves until they can't stand being hungry anymore. The stress and problems in their lives also start to get to them. The tension builds up until they lose control and eat way too much. Eating all that food relaxes them and gets rid of some of the tension, but not for long. Soon they feel guilty about eating so much, and they worry about gaining weight, so they throw up to get rid of all that food.

"Many people with bulimia promise themselves not to throw up again," Cassie said, "but soon the stress in their lives starts getting to them again. They also keep starving themselves. The tension builds up until they're back where they started, about to lose control."

That's kind of what happens to me, Emily realized. She could feel her shoulders relax a little. *But I won't let her know that. I want her to think I'm doing okay now and don't need a counselor. I can handle this by myself.*

"I did throw up a few times," Emily admitted, "but I've stopped now. I just needed to lose a few pounds. I'm still fat compared to most girls at my school. Some of them are *really* skinny. They're the ones everyone should worry about!" Emily hoped she sounded convincing.

"The girls you're thinking of might be really thin because that's the body type they inherited from their parents," Cassie explained. "Or some of them might have anorexia. That's another kind of eating disorder. People with anorexia eat very little, and many of them exercise every minute they can. It doesn't take long for them to look as thin as skeletons.

"On the other hand," she went on, "many people with bulimia weigh about what they should for their height. Others are underweight or even overweight. But all of them are dehydrated and malnourished, so they end up with lots of physical problems, no matter what they weigh. Emily, aren't you a cheerleader?"

Emily nodded, but she hated to be reminded. The regionals were three weeks from Saturday.

"Some cheerleaders and other athletes," Cassie continued, "think they have to keep their weight down so they can do their best, but bulimia makes things worse instead of better. Being dehydrated makes them tired and causes muscle cramps. They often become dizzy and uncoordinated. Their bodies don't have enough water to be able to sweat, so it's harder for them to cool off. Then their bodies start retaining water, so they feel heavy and bloated. Constipation doesn't help either."

Emily stared at the floor. Had Dr. Francis sent a report to Cassie? Did she know that Emily had taken laxatives to lose weight? She hadn't taken any since last week, the day before she fainted, but her body still wasn't working right. Cassie was right about one thing: Emily felt very heavy. Maybe if she took just one or two laxatives, maybe three, she'd feel better.

"So," Cassie went on, "one of our first goals here is for you to stop trying to lose weight and to eat the way you used to. Then most of these physical problems will disappear."

"I *have* been eating more at dinner since I saw Dr. Francis last week," Emily said quickly.

Cassie smiled. "That's a good start. Our goal is for you to eat three healthy, normal meals a day, plus snacks, with no throwing up afterward. As long as you keep throwing up, Emily, you're not only going to feel bad physically, you're also going to feel bad emotionally. Our other major goal is to help you deal with your feelings—learn better ways to handle stress, and just have more fun. Then food won't be so important in your life."

Food will always be important to me, Emily told herself. *It's all I ever think about.*

"So what's fun in your life right now, Emily?" Cassie asked. "Is cheerleading fun?"

Emily sighed. "Not exactly," she admitted. "I thought it would be, but . . . I guess . . . I guess I never should have tried out for cheerleading. I think some of the other cheerleaders wish . . . wish . . . I wasn't on the team." She swallowed hard. "If we lose this big competition that's coming up, it will all be my fault, for sure."

Why did I tell her that? Emily asked herself. *I never told anyone that before! I never said it out loud!* Yet, telling Cassie made her feel a little better, a little less alone.

"So cheerleading is not going well?" Cassie asked.

Emily shook her head. She felt tears gathering in her eyes. *It's hopeless, really hopeless.* "I can't do the cheers right. I'm going to ruin it for the other girls." A tear slid down her cheek, and she brushed it off with the back of her hand.

Cassie handed Emily a tissue. "And the only time you feel anywhere near okay is when you eat a lot, right?"

Emily wiped her face with the tissue and nodded.

Cassie leaned closer to Emily. "Honey, all of us run into problems in our lives. We all make mistakes. We feel disappointed. Sometimes people get angry with us. Sometimes we get angry with them. Everyone has uncomfortable feelings, but you can learn how to handle them without turning to food."

"You mean I should stop eating?" Emily asked. "I tried that. It just makes me want to eat more!"

"I know it does. But to handle those unpleasant feelings, you need to be able to see what's right in your life, along with the problems. People's lives aren't all bad or all good. I'll bet there's a lot of good in your life that you can't see right now. Mostly, you need to be able to talk about your feelings and deal with them instead of trying to bury them under a mountain of food—or get rid of them by vomiting."

"You don't understand!" Emily burst out. "I don't throw up to get rid of my feelings! Every bite I eat turns into fat unless I get rid of it! I have to be very careful of what I eat—and what stays in my body—or I'll blimp up, just like my mother always says!"

Cassie winced. "Well, maybe your mom and I can talk about that sometime soon. Meanwhile, your body has to have food to work right, Emily. Your heart and muscles need certain minerals and the energy that's in food. You get rid of these things when you throw up or take laxatives. That's why you're so tired all the time.

"And your whole body needs more water," Cassie reminded her. "A big part of your blood is water. If your blood doesn't contain enough water, it can't take as much energy and oxygen to your muscles and your brain.

"Emily, the only thing that our bodies turn into fat is any extra calories we eat. But I don't want you to eat too many calories, just well-balanced meals and snacks. That way, your body will get what it really needs."

"If I ate as much as I really need," Emily told her in a tight voice, "I'd weigh three hundred pounds by the end of the first week. That's why I have to throw up! Otherwise, the pounds will start piling on, and I'll look disgusting! I'll be so fat that little kids will point at me!"

"Needing something emotionally is a lot different from needing it physically," Cassie pointed out. "What you think you need and what your body really needs are two different things right now. That's what we'll talk about, you and I. When you start eating the way you used to, you might gain some weight at first, but it'll be the water your body needs and maybe some muscle. It won't be fat."

Emily pushed herself back in her chair, as far as she could get from Cassie. "I knew it! You're going to force me to eat! Wait till you see what happens! Wait till my mother sees me!"

"Emily, you can't be a good cheerleader or do

anything else well unless your body gets the water and energy it needs. No one wants you to get fat, but throwing up and using laxatives is making you sick. It can even kill you if it goes on too long. You're the only one who can stop this, Emily. No one can make you. We can just try to help."

No one can make me, Emily assured herself. *No one.* All she really had to do was make sure Stephanie stopped trying to imitate her. Then everything would be fine. She already had her own life under control. After all, she knew how she felt better than anybody, even the doctor, and for sure this counselor.

Chapter

Fifteen

TOWARD the end of the session, Cassie told Emily about a group of other girls with bulimia who met at the center every Thursday afternoon at three o'clock. "You'll really like this group, Emily," Cassie said. "There are six girls in it now, all your age and a little older. One is a freshman at City College."

Losers probably, Emily told herself. *Girls who never fit in anywhere, like me.* But she told Cassie, "That sounds great, but I have cheerleading practice on Thursdays after school. I've already missed a bunch of practices, so I'll have to work really hard to catch up. I'll go to the group meetings after the regionals are over, okay?"

"Well, I really think you'd like this group," Cassie said, "but I guess you can wait until after the regionals. In the meantime, let's get you started on a balanced eating plan." Emily noticed that Cassie didn't call it a *diet*. "You'll need to meet with the center's dietician, too. Mrs. Mikell comes in every Friday morning. Maybe she'll have time to see you this Friday."

Great, Emily thought. *Someone else trying to take over my life.*

Cassie urged Emily to eat three balanced meals and at least three snacks during the day so she wouldn't feel so hungry in the evening. She asked Emily what she had been eating and suggested some additions, but Emily knew it was way too much food. Cereal with skim milk for breakfast, plus her usual orange and toast. Low-fat dressing on her lunch salad, plus a thermos of soup and a slice of bread with low-fat margarine?

A bottle of fruit juice before cheerleading practice and another one afterward? If Emily were lucky, her fat cells would drown in all that water! And Cassie wanted her to eat a small serving of everything her family was having for dinner! Emily could skip dessert, if she wanted to. Skip dessert. Big deal! On top of that, Cassie suggested a healthy snack during the evening.

Emily agreed to try Cassie's plan, just to keep everyone happy, including her parents. But the counselor also made Emily promise to weigh herself only once a week. Emily knew she couldn't keep that promise. She had to keep checking to make sure she didn't start putting on pounds. If she did, she would have to follow her own "eating plan." She would just have to be very careful so no one caught her.

At the end of the session, Cassie said, "I already have an appointment at this time next week, Emily. Is Tuesday at four o'clock okay for you? If it is, I can see you at that time every week."

Every week—forever? Emily wondered. Her mother said she just had to come once. *I'll say I'll come,* she decided. *Otherwise, Cassie might get angry. Then I'll call on Monday and cancel the appointment.*

"Next Tuesday is okay," Emily said.

As Cassie marked the appointment on a calendar, she said, "I think you know that I'll be sending a report to Dr. Francis every week, right? He wants to know how you're doing."

Emily nodded as if that were no problem. As she waited in the center's living room while her parents talked with Cassie, she decided she'd better come to her next appointment after all. If she didn't, Cassie would tell Dr. Francis. Then he probably would call the school and Mrs. Adams or Mrs. Williams. That would be the end of cheerleading for her.

But what does Dr. Francis expect me to do,

she wondered, *besides come to these appointments? Gain a lot of weight? If I don't, what will happen? Will he call the school anyway?*

I'd better keep Cassie happy, Emily decided, *so she'll send good reports to Dr. Francis. Otherwise, my life is over.*

Emily told her parents she was starting her new eating plan that evening, with a small serving of everything at dinner. It wasn't that different from her usual dinners at home lately, but her mom and dad still looked relieved.

Then Emily made it through the night without getting up to search for food. That was a bigger accomplishment, one her parents would have been proud of, if she had told them. At practice the next afternoon, she did notice that she wasn't as thirsty as usual.

But just as Emily expected, her weight began to creep up. When she got up Friday morning, she weighed 117 1/2! Cassie's wonderful eating plan had made her gain nearly two pounds in less than two days! Cassie and her parents—they just didn't know how her body worked. They were forcing her to eat, but they expected her to stay thin at the same time, like she was magic or something. Emily would have to follow her own plan.

Before going to school Friday morning, she sat quietly through her appointment with the center's dietician, Mrs. Mikell. "Make sure you eat a banana every day to build up your potassium level," Mrs. Mikell said. Something about those electrolytes again. Emily thought a dietician would know that bananas were loaded with calories, but Mrs. Mikell didn't seem to consider that.

With the "help" of Cassie and Mrs. Mikell, Emily figured she would gain more than twenty pounds by the regionals, barely three weeks away. Did the judges take off points for fat cheerleaders? She bet they did.

She hated to think what Becca would say if she saw Emily in her cheerleading uniform after she gained all that weight. Every pleat in that yellow skirt would turn into a fat maroon stripe when Emily tried to zip it over her huge hips and stomach. In fact, her skirt might not fit already, and she had to wear it for the game that night!

So on her way to the cafeteria for lunch, Emily stopped in the restroom. She poured her thermos of soup down the sink and tossed the plastic bag with her slice of bread in the trash. With her stomach growling loudly, Emily was tempted to eat the extra food and then throw up, but someone might catch her. Anyway, she figured throwing it out was easier on her body. Gotta keep those electrolytes, you know.

Jodi found her at lunch again, even though Emily sat back in a corner of the cafeteria.

"There you are!" Jodi said as she settled herself at Emily's table. Then she pulled her lunch and a plastic bag of cookies out of her book bag. "I made these last night. They're oatmeal and everything! Oatmeal's real good for you, you know."

The cookies smelled so warm and spicy that Emily almost snatched them from Jodi and stuffed them all in her mouth.

"Ummm, no thanks, Jodi. I . . . I have to go now. I have to . . . uhh . . . make up a math test I missed last week." Emily grabbed her salad container and soda can and almost ran out of the cafeteria, before she could lose control.

As she sat in class that afternoon, Emily's stomach screamed for more food. She wondered if eating more lately had somehow made her hunger pains stronger. Maybe her stomach was mad at her for teasing it with more food. *Get used to being empty again,* she told it. *You are not getting all that food anymore. You'll just turn it into disgusting fat.*

By the time cheerleading practice was over that afternoon, Emily was desperately hungry. As she pedaled home, she hoped no one would be there so she could raid the refrigerator or the pantry. But she got home just as her mother did—with pizza she had picked up for dinner. Her dad was already there and had made a salad to balance out the meal. They were eating early so Emily could get to the football game on time.

"Isn't that your fifth slice, Emily?" her father asked. "I think you ate more than I did tonight. You're definitely getting better!"

Emily smiled and nodded. *Just don't watch me too closely after dinner, Dad.*

"We're glad you're eating so much, honey," her mother mumbled, but Emily knew she wasn't glad at all.

Suddenly Emily realized that Stephanie was staring at her. Her sister had been talking nonstop about some boy on her bus, but now she said, "You sure are eating a lot, Emily."

Emily felt a chill. She knew Stephanie was going to watch her after dinner. It was going to be really hard to get rid of all that pizza.

Fortunately, she didn't have to throw up in the bathroom. While Stephanie was loading the dishwasher, Emily took the empty pizza box out to the garbage can beside the garage. In the can, she found some stale bread in a plastic bag. Emily quickly threw up in the bag, on top of the bread. The rotting smell from the other garbage made it easy to barf. Then she reclosed the bag with its twist tie and pushed it under other trash in the can.

It was nearly dark, so Emily was fairly sure none of the neighbors saw her. Soon the night wind would take away the smell. No one would know.

Emily went back to the kitchen and got some breath mints from her purse. As she slipped them in her mouth, Stephanie said, "I'll come up while you get dressed for the game, okay?"

Emily knew the real reason her sister was coming upstairs, but she smiled and said, "Sure!"

As they passed the upstairs bathroom, Stephanie whispered, "I'm glad you didn't go in there after dinner, Emily. I was a little worried. After all that pizza, I thought you might . . . you know . . ."

Emily hugged her, making sure not to breathe in her face. "Nah! I don't do that any more. That was good pizza, wasn't it?"

Stephanie grinned and nodded.

I've got things under control again, Emily thought. *I'll just have to be more imaginative about where I throw up. After all, they can't watch me every minute.*

Emily was really thirsty and had a headache during most of the game that night. And she had to struggle to finish a handspring after Sycamore made its only touchdown.

Still, her cheerleading skirt fit fine.

Chapter

Sixteen

ON Saturday morning, Emily was down to 116 pounds, thank goodness. Her stomach was upset, and she was still thirsty, but she knew she could live with that. She was pouring her daily bowl of cereal when her mom came into the kitchen. "Want some?" Emily asked.

"Uhhh, not just yet," Mrs. Davis answered. "I'm really not hungry now. Maybe later."

Just staying trim, Emily thought as she sliced a banana into her bowl of corn crisps.

But as soon as Emily was alone in the kitchen, she poured what was left in her bowl—most of it—into the disposal in the sink. She didn't turn it on because the noise would give her away. Emily figured no one would notice the cereal and banana slices under the rubber flap covering the disposal. They would disappear completely the next time someone turned it on.

Then Emily asked her dad to drop her at the animal shelter on his way to do some errands. During the game the night before, she had promised Jodi that she would help for a while. *See?* she told herself, *I do keep some of my promises—as long as there's no food involved.* By helping at the shelter, she could also prove to Jodi that she was doing okay now, that no one needed to worry about her— or bug her to eat.

Jodi had said she didn't think Evan would be there, but she must have had her fingers crossed, Emily decided.

As soon as Emily came in the back door of the shelter, Evan called, "Hi!" He was in the kitchen, holding the leashes of two half-grown shepherd-mix dogs. They were eagerly tugging him toward the door so they could go for a walk.

"How long will you be here?" he asked. She smiled and shrugged, so he said, "Stay till I have a chance to talk to you, okay?"

As the dogs pulled Evan out the door, Emily wondered if he knew about her "problem." Jodi and Evan were good friends, so she might have told him. But he must not know, she decided, because he looked as if he was actually glad to see her.

Just then, Jodi came into the shelter kitchen. "Hi, Em! Want to feed the kittens and everything this morning?" It turned out that "and everything" meant cleaning out their litter boxes, which tired Emily more than she had expected.

Evan was soon back from walking the dogs and hurried upstairs to help with the kittens. Emily recognized a few of the little cats from her first visit, and Evan filled her in on how the others had gotten to the shelter. Fortunately, Snickers had found a home. Emily hoped he was happy there.

When she opened the cage of a little black kitten, it leaned against her hand and purred loudly. She picked it up and petted its silky fur.

"I'd sure like to take you home with me," she murmured, half to herself.

"Do you have any pets at home?" Evan asked.

It was hard to think with him standing so close. "No, but if our family ever got a cat, I think it would be pure-bred, not one like this, from an animal shelter."

"Why?" he asked.

"Because . . . because it would have to be a special cat of some kind, something my mom could brag about to her friends."

Evan thought for a minute. "Is that what

your mom said?"

Emily laughed. "No, she wouldn't just come out and say it, but I know her." Suddenly Emily was starving. She wished she had eaten more of her cereal that morning instead of pouring it out.

"How do you feel now, Emily?" Evan asked quietly. "Jodi told me you had the flu or something last week."

The flu? What a relief!

"I'm fine now. Thanks for . . . for helping me that day," she mumbled.

"That's okay! The hard part was fighting off the four other guys who wanted to carry you," he told her with a grin.

Emily's face caught fire.

"Emily!" Jodi called from downstairs. "Your dad's here to pick you up."

"Already?" Evan caught her arm. "Don't go, Emily. I'll give you a ride home later, whenever you want to go!"

Emily felt his strong fingers circling her arm. She gently pulled free and headed for the stairs. "Thanks, but I gotta go. I'll see you at school on Monday." Emily had asked her father to stop and get her after he finished his errands. She knew that wouldn't allow her much time at the shelter, but it was long enough, as it turned out.

Saturday night, Emily baby-sat for the neighbors again and found more food that she didn't think they would miss. The more she thought about Evan's hand on her arm, the more she ate. She was careful to clean up all the evidence afterward, in the kitchen and in the bathroom.

By Monday afternoon's cheerleading practice, Emily was feeling a little light-headed. She had been back down to 115 3/4 that morning, since she stopped drinking all that milk and soup and juice. But she had just missed a hand movement during the dance section of the routine, so Mrs. Williams was making them all do it again.

Emily heard their groans, but being dizzy make it hard to think. Moving fast made the dizziness worse. The second time through the dance, Emily got a cramp in her left calf. She did her best to finish the routine without letting anyone know. Emily was careful not to look at Jodi, but she could feel Jodi's eyes on her. After practice, she purposely drank a bottle of juice in front of Jodi, in case she was getting suspicious.

That night Emily lay in bed thinking about cheerleading practice that afternoon. The other girls had been really annoyed with her. Even Mrs. Williams seemed a little impatient. The more she thought about it, the hungrier she got.

Finally, Emily slipped down to the kitchen and found a can of beef stew and a box of saltines. She opened the can with an old hand-operated opener because she knew the electric one might wake everyone up. A few minutes later, she felt much better, even though the stew had been cold, but she still needed more food. After more searching, she came up with three cans of tuna and one of fruit cocktail. Her hand hurt from using the old can opener, but at last she felt full. Then it was time to visit the bathroom.

When she got up Tuesday morning, Emily's stomach was upset again and her head hurt, as usual, but she was still at 115 3/4. Then another worry hit her. Maybe Cassie would weigh her during her appointment that afternoon.

A nurse had weighed her at Dr. Francis's office, and Emily figured he had sent a report to Cassie. She had seen the nurse write 116 on her chart, about what she weighed now. Was that okay? Or would they expect to see all those extra pounds she had started to put on because of her new "eating plan"?

Just in case, Emily ate most of her cereal for breakfast, along with toast and a banana. She even ate her thermos of soup with her salad at lunch, but threw away her bread. No point in overdoing it.

Jodi ate lunch with her, as usual. Emily had told Jodi about her appointment that afternoon, but she had been careful to keep the details of her new "eating plan" to herself. All she needed was Jodi wondering what happened to her slice of bread.

All through cheerleading practice, Emily couldn't stop worrying about the weigh-in. She was so distracted that she made several mistakes during the dance. Emily could feel the angry looks from the other girls, but she couldn't get the appointment out of her mind.

About fifteen minutes before the end of practice, Emily asked Mrs. Williams if she could leave early for an appointment. "Of course," the coach said quickly.

Anything to get rid of me, Emily guessed. She hurried into the locker room and got on the scale. Only 115 1/2! She must have sweated off a quarter of a pound during practice!

After getting dressed, Emily took off on her bike toward the mental health center. She had told her parents the night before that they didn't need to give her a ride. She would be on time for her appointment. She promised.

Maybe I should stop at a store and buy a can of soda, she thought. *If I drink it before I*

159

get to the center, it might add a whole pound.

The closer Emily got to the center, the more she worried. Soon she was trembling. Could Cassie tell how much Emily had really been eating? Would she know that Emily had thrown up Friday night after eating the pizza? And Saturday at the neighbors'? And last night, too? Would Cassie tell her parents and Dr. Francis? They would never trust her again!

Emily stopped her bike at a corner. *I don't need this,* she decided. *I don't need a counselor. I could control my life just fine if everyone would just leave me alone. I'm not going to the center. It's no one else's business how much I weigh, and that includes Cassie and Dr. Francis.*

She couldn't go back to cheerleading practice, though. Jodi knew about the appointment. She would wonder why Emily came back so soon and she'd ask a million questions. Emily couldn't go home yet either. If Stephanie was there, she might remember that this was the afternoon for Emily to see the counselor. But Emily could go to the animal shelter—they always needed help.

It took her about ten minutes to get there on her bike. An elderly woman named Mrs. Denzer was working at the shelter that afternoon. She said she would be glad to have

Emily's help with the animals.

After feeding and watering several kittens, Emily took the little black one out of its cage. "I really hope someone gives you a good home pretty soon," she whispered. "You deserve some-one to love you." For some reason, her eyes filled with tears.

Just then she heard footsteps on the stair-way. They seemed too heavy for Mrs. Denzer. Suddenly a blond head appeared at the top of the steps.

"Emily!" Evan said with a big smile. "You're here! That's great!" Then he turned and yelled down the steps. "Jodi, Emily's here!"

Chapter

Seventeen

WHILE Evan helped with the kittens, he talked on and on about something funny that had happened in his French class. Emily wasn't listening. She was waiting to hear Jodi's footsteps on the stairs. What could Emily possibly say to her? More empty promises?

Soon Emily and Evan were giving the last kitten food and water. Jodi still hadn't come upstairs.

"Maybe you can help me walk some of the dogs today," Evan told Emily as he closed the last cage. "It's really nice out so . . ." Then he glanced at her face. Evan quickly put his hand on her arm. "What's wrong? Are you going to faint again?"

She shook her head. *But I wish I could,* she thought. *In fact, I wish I could disappear.* She couldn't, though, just like she couldn't stay upstairs all afternoon.

"I'm fine, Evan. Let's go walk the dogs." With feet as heavy as cement, Emily started toward the stairs.

Jodi wasn't in the shelter's living room. Mrs. Denzer's coat had been lying across an empty cage, and now it was gone, so Emily guessed she had gone home. Maybe, she prayed, Jodi did, too. Maybe she didn't even hear Evan yell down the stairs that I was here.

"The leashes are in the kitchen," Evan said as he led Emily past the cages of meowing cats and yipping puppies.

There was Jodi, sitting at the beat-up kitchen table with her back to them. She was looking out a streaked window at the muddy backyard. Emily swallowed hard. What could she say?

Evan took a handful of leashes off a hook on the wall. "We're going to walk a couple of the dogs, Jodi. Want to come?"

Jodi turned to face them. Her face was red and puffy. "I guess you missed your appointment and everything, right, Emily?"

Emily's heart sank. Jodi really did care about her, and Emily had let her down, along with a lot of other people.

Evan hurried over to Jodi. "What appointment? What's the matter, Jodi?" He looked back at Emily and then at Jodi. "What's going on here? Tell me what's wrong with you two!"

Jodi covered her face with her hands and started to cry. Her breathing came in gasps, and her shoulders shook.

Emily hurried over and put her arm around Jodi's shoulders. "I'm sorry, Jodi. Really, really sorry." Now Emily's eyes burned, too. "I'll go next week, I promise." Emily sighed. "I mean it this time, Jodi. For sure. I'll go."

"Go where?" Evan asked anxiously. "What's so important?"

Ignoring him, Jodi wiped her face on her sleeve and looked up at Emily. "And what will happen between your appointments, Emily? Will you keep slowly killing yourself?"

Emily could see that Jodi hadn't been fooled at all.

"Killing yourself?" Evan stared at Emily. "What does she mean? Tell me what's going on!" he nearly shouted. Then he grabbed Emily's hand. "Are you really sick, Emily? Is that why you fainted before?"

Suddenly Evan's face turned pale. "Oh, I hope you're not sick, Emmy. I hope not," he whispered.

Evan put his arms around Emily and held her close. Surrounded by his strong, warm arms, she could feel his heart beating under his shirt. She felt so safe in those arms, but she knew she didn't belong there.

Emily gently pushed him back. "I'm not sick. Not really," she said quietly. "I'll be okay."

"I've heard that before," Jodi said in a choked voice.

With one hand, Evan tilted Emily's face up so he could see her eyes. "You're not acting like you're okay. And I can see that Jodi's really worried. If there's something wrong with you, Emily, I want to help. I'll do anything I can to help you."

He traced the swollen glands under her jaw with his finger. "Is this part of the problem? Do you have some kind of cancer or something? Tell me the truth, Emily! Are you sick?"

Am I sick? Emily asked herself. She thought about getting up in the middle of the night to wolf down every bit of food she could find. She thought about sneaking outside to throw up in the garbage can.

There was so little water in her body now that she barely had enough for tears. Still, her feet and ankles were swollen. She always had an open sore on one knuckle. Her jaw was so puffy that she looked as if she had just had a bunch of teeth pulled.

On top of that, she was always weak and tired. And dizzy. Even now Emily was worried that Evan would smell barf on her breath. And her throat hurt, the sores in her mouth hurt, her head hurt, her stomach hurt . . .

Am I sick? I guess so. I sure feel sick. Then she remembered something Cassie had told her: "You're the only one who can stop this, Emily."

It was time—time to stop fooling herself about being in control. Her life had never been more out of control than it was right now. And she had never felt more miserable or more scared. Or more alone.

"I guess I am sick," she told Evan quietly. "But I don't have cancer or anything like that. I think I can get better. Maybe. With some help. The only problem is, I'll get fat, too." She blinked back tears. "And I won't be a cheerleader anymore."

Evan pulled her close again. "I really, really like you, Emily Davis. I don't care how much you weigh. And while you're getting better, Emmy, I wish you would let me spend some time with you. Maybe you could get to like me, too."

He kissed her gently on the forehead. Suddenly Emily didn't want to disappear anymore.

"But I won't be a cheerleader anymore . . ."

"So what?" he said. "No one's a cheerleader forever."

Emily hadn't thought about it that way. She wasn't much of a cheerleader now, anyway. It wasn't a lot to give up. She smiled and asked, "What time is it?"

Evan glanced at his watch. "About a quarter to five."

"Would you give me a ride?" Emily asked him. Then she turned to Jodi. "You can come, too, Jodi. I hope you will." She smiled again. "I want you both to meet a new friend of mine. Her name is Cassie."

On the way to the center, Emily was so nervous about facing Cassie that her hands shook, but when she got there, the counselor wasn't angry with her after all. After meeting Jodi and Evan, Cassie asked Emily to stay and talk for a few minutes, although her appointment time had passed. Evan left to take Jodi home.

Emily began by admitting, through her tears, why she had almost not come: she was afraid Cassie would weigh her and figure out that Emily had thrown up again and again since her first appointment, despite her promises to everyone.

Cassie just smiled and shook her head. First, she explained that she had never intended to weigh Emily. "It doesn't matter how much you weigh," she said. "It just matters that you are eating the kinds and amounts of food you need—and not abusing your body by vomiting or using laxatives.

"In fact," Cassie told her, "gaining weight is not necessarily a sign that you are getting well. Some people who continue to binge and throw up actually gain weight. A lot of the calories they eat during their binges are absorbed by their bodies even though they try to get rid of them by throwing up.

"After you start eating healthy meals, Emily, your body will soon get back to normal and find its natural weight. But I really don't think you'll gain twenty pounds, like you thought." Cassie grinned. "And I do think your cheerleading skirt will still fit okay. Well, maybe just a little maroon will show in those pleats. But you can live with that, right?"

Emily nodded, but she knew Cassie would probably have to tell her parents and Dr. Francis that Emily had tried to fool them all. Dr. Francis would contact the school, and that would be the end of cheerleading. Fitting into that skirt wouldn't matter.

Still, her two good friends, Evan and Jodi, didn't care whether she was a cheerleader. They liked her just as she was. That was enough for her right now. In fact, that was more than she had ever hoped for.

"As long as you eat right from now on,"

Cassie was saying, "you'll probably do okay in the regionals. You won't be outstanding because you really have abused your body—but you'll do okay. The other cheerleaders won't have anything to complain about."

Emily gasped. "You won't tell anyone what . . . what I've been doing? That I nearly missed this appointment? I can still be a cheerleader? What if I go past the weight limit?"

Cassie smiled. "Emily, some people just need extra time before they decide to make important changes. I know you'll be tempted to throw up again, especially when things get tense. You might do it, too. But we'll keep talking, you and I, until you feel more comfortable with your new-old eating style—and with yourself! And those meetings on Thursdays with the other girls will help a lot.

"By the way, Emily, the schools in this county aren't allowed to weigh cheerleaders anymore. There is no weight limit."

Emily's mouth fell open. "But I thought . . ."

"I would have told you if you had mentioned it before," Cassie said and smiled kindly. "I didn't know you were worried about that. Talking is a good thing, you know!"

Cassie promised she would talk some more with Emily's mom about the importance of being fit and healthy, but not necessarily thin.

Emily thought that would help Stephanie, too.

* * * * *

The next day at lunch time, Emily was finishing her soup when Jodi sat down beside her in the cafeteria.

"Too bad Evan eats during the other lunch period and everything," Jodi teased. "I miss him, don't you?"

Emily grinned. She still couldn't believe he liked her so much. He had asked her again to go to the movies with him this Saturday. It hadn't taken her long to say "yes," as long as they didn't eat anything. She didn't think she was ready to eat in front of him yet. Maybe she would after she had more time to talk with Cassie.

As Jodi got out her lunch, Emily started on her salad, with dressing now, and ate her slice of bread.

"Oatmeal cookie?" Jodi held up a bag of them.

Emily grinned. "I'd love one."

"You can have them all!"

Emily shook her head. "No, one will be perfect." She chose a small one and ate it all. She knew she could have another one—or the whole bag—if she wanted it, but today one was enough.

On their way out of the cafeteria, Emily noticed that Jodi suddenly seemed tense. Then she realized why. Emily laughed and poked her friend with her elbow.

"You don't have to worry, Jodi. I'm not going to make a break for the restroom. I know my body needs everything I just ate. I've got to build myself up for those regionals because Evan is going to come and watch. Besides, throwing up is really and truly DISGUSTING!"

Jodi grinned at her. "You're right, you know."

They walked out of the cafeteria with their arms around each other's waists.

For More Information

Eating disorders among girls and women in the United States are more common than most people realize. If you or someone you care about is struggling with either bulimia or anorexia, please let someone know. You might consider telling a school nurse or guidance counselor. These disorders can be life-threatening. Don't hesitate to call for information or help.

For more information, contact:
National Eating Disorders Organization
6655 South Yale Avenue
Tulsa, OK 74136-3329
(918) 481-4044

For help in your community, look in the Yellow Pages of your phone book under "Eating Disorders" or "Counseling."

About the Author

"Bulimia and anorexia are so common now that starving and throwing up almost seem normal," says Linda Barr. "But these eating disorders aren't just about losing weight. Most of these girls are trying to deal with the pressures of growing up. Once they find a healthier way to do that—and give up their deadly secret—they'll be on their way to a happier life."

In her seven books for Willowisp Press, Linda Barr has focused on problems that directly affect young people. She hopes that learning about how others deal with these problems will encourage some of her readers to seek help. And other readers will better understand the struggles their friends are facing.

Mrs. Barr lives in Westerville, Ohio, with her husband Tom, daughter Colleen, and a parrot named Sunny. Her son Dan and his wife Amy live nearby.